Singl

Copyright

Copyright © 2022 by Worth a Read Too, LLC.

United States of America.

All rights reserved. No part of this book may be reproduced in any manner without written permission of the copyright owner except for the use of quotations in a book review or academic paper so long as the book is cited.

To request permission, email selysrivera@worthareadtoo.com.

ISBN:

979-8-9863324-4-4 (eBook)

979-8-9863324-3-7 (Paperback)

Originally published November 1, 2022 by Worth a Read Too, LLC.

Cover Design by Selys Rivera using Canva.

To the BookTok community.

I don't know how you do it, but y'all somehow manage to both inspire me to write and make me feel guilty for not writing enough. I also both blame and thank you for making my TBR list impossible to finish.

This one's for you, my BookTok besties!

Praise

"I TRULY LOVED THIS story and every single one of the characters! I found the portrayal of these relationships and their growing friendship to be extremely heartwarming, realistic and relevant." - Amanda Rodrigues, Author*

⟨ ⟩

"IT'S HEARTWARMING IN general, but the ending particularly so." - Anthony Woodside, Writer*

⟨ ⟩

"IT FELT LIKE BEING in high school again and re-living an interesting night out with a great group of friends." - S.C. Muir, Author*

⟨ ⟩

*RECEIVED A COPY FROM the author in the hopes of an honest review.

Disclaimer

This is a work of fiction. While the author has pulled inspiration from the experiences in her life, the characters and events of the story are imaginary. Any resemblance to actual persons, living or dead, or actual events is purely coincidental and will probably be as surprising to the author as they would be to the reader.

⟨ ⟩

There are references to pop culture to help the story feel more relatable. However, these are neither endorsement nor defamation. Lastly, the characters in this book have minds of their own. Therefore, their opinions may not match the author's, despite her best efforts to convince them otherwise.

Content Warning

IF YOU'VE READ EITHER of my last two books, you'll know I believe in trigger warnings. I wouldn't want to read a book that reminds me of something I want to forget. So, why should you?

However, with the lighthearted nature of this book, I'm happy to say that the trigger warnings are minor. So much so that I referred to this section as Content Warning instead.

But you have the right to know what you're getting into.

So, here is what you should know about this book:

- Homophobia & Transphobia (including misgendering)
- Learning Disability & Mental Health
- Racism & Xenophobia
- Sexual References
- Swearing / Cussing
- Unhealthy Relationships

If it helps, I think you'll be proud of how the main characters of this book handle each of these situations.

Hope to see you on the other side!

Chapter 1: Duri

"SINGLE RIDER!" THE ride attendant points a somewhat wrinkled index finger towards Duri and then gestures at the next person in the regular line. "You two. Row 3."

Duri pauses the podcast episode of *Sit and Kick* she'd been listening to and takes her time putting her wireless earbuds back in their case. The ride attendant gives her an impatient look. Duri rolls her brown eyes and stuffs both the case and her smartphone into her front pockets.

She steps toward the guy she'll have to wait at the gate with until it opens for them to get on the ride. She sighs, reminding herself it's a small price to pay to get on her favorite roller coaster sooner.

Black Hole Planet is Duri's guilty pleasure. She knows she should've grown out of it, especially after middle school. That's when she realized she's less of a space geek and more of a sports enthusiast. All things space related took a back seat once she discovered her passion for track and field in high school.

It was a slippery slope from there as that led to attending school soccer games, watching the Super Bowl, following the Olympics, and keeping track of everything the Orlando Magic did.

Okay, so some might call that passion an obsession.

Still, whenever Duri is *really* upset, it's comforting to remember simpler times. Like when she was twelve. Back then, her biggest worry was doing all her chores, so her parents would take her and her twin sister to Black Hole Planet for their birthday.

Hana also eventually fell out of love with the amusement park as she changed once she began high school. Except she found a passion for dance, being popular, and getting straight As so their parents would worship at her feet.

But Duri doesn't want to think about Hana right now. She's why Duri faked a cold to get out of church and sneak out to the park. And while Duri doesn't *mind* church, she also doesn't feel like being stuck with her sister after last night.

They'd gotten into another one of their arguments over college. Again. Because Duri should've picked her major by now. Duri should aim higher than community college. She should try to improve her life. Not just run around and get sweaty with girls.

Blah. Blah.

Honestly, Duri can't even remember how the argument started, or who started it. All she remembers is standing furiously in the hallway in front of her and Hana's rooms. Words escaping Duri's lips as fast as she could regret them. Hana fighting back, her words cutting just as deadly.

And who did their parents side with? Hana.

Their annoyingly perfect daughter. The daughter who can actually speak fluent Korean and teaches Sunday school to the little kids at church and probably reads to the blind whenever she's not out partying with her friends. Surprise, surprise.

Not.

Duri runs a hand through her straight, dark brunette bob of hair as she finally gets a good look at who she's being paired with. When she recognizes him, she stops so quickly that her sneaker catches on the concrete. She almost trips but catches herself at the last second.

Before the guy can see her—at least she hopes he hasn't seen her yet—she spins around. She can't even bring herself to risk a glance over her shoulder to check if he caught her.

Irritated, the ride attendant asks, "Is there a problem, Miss?"

His eyelids droop over his grayish blue eyes as he waits for her response.

"You could say that," Duri says, low enough for only the attendant to hear. She's close enough to read his name tag. "Okay, look. Matt, you can't pair me with that guy."

Shifting his weight from one foot to the other, Matt lets out an exasperated sigh that practically spells out "I don't get paid enough for this".

"And why not?"

Duri takes a deep breath and then rushes through her explanation.

"Because he's the son of the pastor of my church and I ditched worship today and he'll totally give me away and I don't have time to explain this more, but I really need to just *not* ride with him, okay?"

Matt's face is the picture of boredom. That's the only response Duri gets. She lets out her own exasperated sigh as her eyes flick back to the other single riders. She sprints to the next person in line, waving her hands frantically to get his attention.

When he turns towards her, Duri tries to channel her inner game show host. She gestures towards the ride with a sweeping motion of her arm. And with mock enthusiasm, she exclaims, "It's your lucky day! You can ride before me."

Chapter 2: Alex

IT TAKES ALEX A FEW moments before they're out of their nostalgic reverie. They hadn't been paying attention to what was around them, robotically moving through the line as their mind wandered repeatedly back to *him*.

After all, that's what today's visit to the park is about.

Alex, of course, can't get over their high school sweetheart, so instead they torture themselves with memories of their ex. And the best place to do *that* is on Galactic Survival, Ben's favorite ride at Black Hole Planet.

A huge sci-fi nerd, Ben is a big fan of the dual spaceship style roller coaster trains that simulate a battle with plenty of exciting loops and drops. Alex has to admit that the ride isn't half bad, considering it was made in the nineties. It also has a retro fifties vibe that they can appreciate.

Their favorite part is when the rollercoaster goes into a replica of the moon.

The inside must be filled with black lights because out of the darkness glows not only the fake stars and other planets simulating the Milky Way but also whatever riders wear that is white or light colored. The orchestra style soundtrack on the ride complements the action well too. Alex likes to listen to the latest hits, but they have to admit the ride's music is well done.

After getting off the ride, Ben always used to say, "Totally gets your heart pumping, right?"

"Maybe," Alex would reply coyly. "But I don't need a roller coaster for that." And then they'd kiss their boyfriend on his perfectly pink and soft lips.

At least, that's what used to happen.

"Hello!" The exasperated voice belongs to a fair skinned stranger trying to get Alex's attention.

Alex blinks a few times as their vision focuses back to the present. As they do so, their eyes catch on the person's cute pink belt. The color of the roses Ben got them for Valentine's Day.

Sigh.

"Sorry!" Alex replies, shaking their head. They meant it in a gesture of clarification, as if trying to shake out all the junk that's cluttering their thoughts.

But it must seem like they declined whatever they had just been asked because Rose Belt begs, "Please, *please*, switch places with me."

"Oh!" Alex exclaims, finally understanding. "Yeah, that's fine."

"Thank you! You're a lifesaver. You have no idea what this means to me."

Alex shrugs. "It's really NBD."

They step around Rose Belt, who steps back into the single rider line. If Alex weren't already so distracted by their thoughts, they might've taken a moment to stare back quizzically. It probably isn't a good sign when someone is *that* eager to switch. But they don't have the energy to figure it out. So they just roll with it.

"Great," says the ride attendant in the fakest chipper voice Alex has ever heard. "Row 3."

Alex turns to greet whoever the ride attendant paired them with. Then they almost choke. Ben doesn't need to turn away from his conversation with his parents. Alex would recognize that mop of strawberry blonde hair anywhere.

It's just Alex's luck, though, because he turns away from his parents. Ben locks eyes with his ex-partner, who is standing paralyzed just a few feet away. But Alex barely has time to gasp before Ben has already gone back to his conversation. As if nothing had happened. As if his ex never existed.

As if Alex is no one.

But they know Ben's tells. His eyes widen, just barely. One muscle in his jaw moves when he grits his teeth. He shifts uncomfortably from one foot to the other and back again. Alex has seen them all before. And Alex just saw them all again.

Turning around so fast that they almost slip out of one of their violet ballet flats, Alex rushes back to the person they agreed to switch with.

The ride attendant mutters, "What now?"

Ignoring the comment, Alex speaks in a loud whisper. "I changed my mind."

Clearly startled, Rose Belt seems taken aback for a second. Then, just as quickly, they reply, "Oh, come on!" They raise their hands in the air helplessly. "Why? Don't tell me you're also trying to avoid the pastoral family from the church you ditched today."

"What?" Alex replies, perfectly shaped eyebrows meeting in the middle. They shake their head. "No, I'm Jewish. I go to synagogue on—that's not the point! I didn't skip church, but I *am* trying to avoid *him.*" They point a manicured thumb back in the direction where Ben must still be talking with his parents.

"You too?" Rose Belt looks surprised, but nods in understanding. "All right."

Alex is about to ask what that meant. But then a deep, breathy voice interrupts.

"One of you," says the ride attendant sternly. "Row 3. Now."

"Wait," Alex pleads as they read the ride attendant's name tag. "Matt. Just one second. Please."

"Hey," Rose Belt hisses at the next person in line. A golden brown skinned teenager about a foot shorter than Alex. When the teen doesn't look up from their smartphone, Rose Belt tries again. "Hey, you."

No reply.

Alex tries a different approach. "Excuse me."

Still no response. The person just continues to bite the cuticle of their pinky and stares at the screen of their phone.

"Hey!" Rose Belt is louder this time, showing the desperation that Alex feels inside. "Chick in the purple fairy dress. Help us out, will you?"

Chapter 3: Jaya

"YOU REALLY SHOULDN'T assume people's gender."

"Seriously? That's what you're worried about right now."

"I mean, there's no need to be *rude*."

"Ugh! Fine. *Person* in the purple fairy dress. Help us out, will you?"

That's when Jaya realizes the two people in front of the line are talking to *her* and not to someone else, like she originally assumed. She looks up abruptly, her already naturally big hazel eyes widening even further.

An East Asian girl in blue jeans and a cream-colored t-shirt stands alongside a rather effeminate looking guy with sepia brown skin. Both appear to be in their late teens like Jaya. Both stare back at her.

"Uh," she starts quietly, then begins again with a bit more confidence. "Can I help you?"

Jaya just about jumps out of her skin when both the girl and guy rush to her, each grabbing hold of one of her arms. She doesn't mind being touched. Actually, she quite enjoys physical affection with her family. Like cuddling with her mom while watching T.V. or playfully wrestling her brother for the video game controller that doesn't have a missing button. She even likes the long bear hugs her dad gives her.

But she doesn't know these people.

The guy seems to notice Jaya's discomfort first as he lets go almost immediately. He nudges the girl, who follows suit. Both apologize quickly before explaining their odd behavior.

"You have to be next," says the girl.

"Right," agrees the guy. "Because I can't take this one's place." He bumps an elbow against the girl's arm.

"And I can't go," continues the girl. "So it has to be you."

Jaya raises one of her thick eyebrows as she puts her phone away. "Uh, why?"

She leans over to see who they would pair her with. All she notices is a seemingly attractive white guy with reddish blonde hair, glasses, and a t-shirt that has a sci-fi character on the front. She briefly wonders what show it's from.

Her younger brother, Karib, loves sci-fi so he'd probably know. In fact, Jaya is only in the park today because he won first place at his school's science fair. And he always asks to go to Black Hole Planet for special occasions.

If she remembers correctly, Karib's actually wearing a character from the same show on his t-shirt right now. She makes a mental note to ask him later.

She ventures to ask now, "What's wrong with him?"

"Nothing!"

"Well," the other girl disagrees, "I'm not getting into that. Let's just say we have very good reasons not to ride with him."

Just then, someone with a feminine voice shouts, "What's taking so long?!"

An avid avoider of conflict, Jaya immediately winces.

Another person shouts with a nasal voice, "Just pick someone already!"

"All right, kids." The manly voice comes from the ride attendant standing behind the two strangers. According to his name tag, his name is Matt. "The crowd's getting restless. Don't make me ask again."

He seems tired, if the bags under his eyes are any sign. Jaya can also see his gray hair is no doubt unbrushed under the space helmet of his costume. His salt and pepper beard isn't that well groomed, either.

"Just five more minutes," replies the girl.

"Lady, you ain't gettin' five more *seconds*," responds Matt. His voice is sharp, losing the somewhat professional tone Jaya heard him use earlier with other park patrons in line. Nodding his head towards someone in the regular line, he adds, "Maybe you should just get back in line with your parents."

The girl scrunches up her button nose. "My parents?"

Jaya's gaze follows the direction Matt indicated. Behind the guy in the regular line stands a Caucasian couple, who she assumes are his parents. But Matt was looking behind them at an East Asian couple. They're chatting away, only glancing occasionally at the drama happening mere feet away. Jaya can barely hear them.

"Wow," the girl says. "Did you just assume they're my parents because we're the only Asian people near the front of the lines?" She shakes her head in disgust and the guy joins her.

"That's messed up."

The girl scoffs as she crosses her arms in front of her almost flat chest. "I don't even know what language they're speaking."

"Japanese," Jaya surprises herself by chiming in. The guy raises both his perfectly tweezed eyebrows at her, pleasantly surprised.

"That's impressive. How did you know that?"

Jaya shrugs. "I used to be really into manga and anime. But I'm not fluent or anything. I only picked out a few words."

"Nice!"

He gives her a blindingly beautiful smile, all straight white teeth and healthy gums. Jaya can't help but offer back her own smile. That kind of demeanor is contagious.

The other girl nods in agreement to the side conversation between her companions, though her gaze never leaves Matt's less than thrilled face.

"I can't speak Korean for shit, but I can understand it. So, I can confirm she's right. See? Not my parents."

Matt's light complexion flushes red before he takes off his open helmet. He holds it under the crook of one arm so he can rub the palm of his other hand on his face. He lets out a frustrated groan before smacking his hand on the plastic dome of the helmet. The resounding thwack startles all three teens, but most of all Jaya. She's so easily scared that she still refuses to even watch *Goosebumps* movies.

"Get out of my line," Matt growls.

"What?!" exclaim the three teenagers.

"But we didn't do anything!"

"Sir, uh, I don't think..."

"What the literal f—"

"Is there a problem here?"

The last question, spoken in a high-pitched southern accent, comes from a female security guard who appears out of nowhere. Jaya isn't sure who called for security. But she sees other people are noticing the antics of the group.

Pointed fingers. Annoyed glances. Entertained smiles. She even watches some pull out phones to record, presumably for social media.

Jaya swallows hard. She doesn't enjoy being the center of attention, especially in crowds. Her face feels hotter than the Central Florida sun outside. Her eyes dart between her companions.

The guy appears almost as shocked as her, but the girl isn't facing Jaya. Instead, the girl stares at the beginning of the regular line. Then, suddenly, she grabs Jaya's hand, as well as the guy's.

And they run.

Chapter 4: Duri

DURI SPRINTS THROUGH the single rider line back to the entrance of the ride. The guy that she originally asked to switch, and the girl with the thick brown wavy hair, stumble behind their leader.

Other single riders in line move out of the way quickly. They try to press against the railings that separate them from the other lines. The regular line is on one side. The Shooting Star line on the other. That one's for those lucky park guests who pay extra to get on rides faster.

However, not everyone moves away fast enough. Shoulders bump into shoulders more than once. Clasped hands sometimes graze a sweaty arm. People cry out in surprise or shout in annoyance as the teens pass by, but Duri ignores them.

She knows how to block the outside world by focusing on her breaths and pace. Her instincts try to kick in—her lungs naturally picking their rhythm, her feet finding the perfect purchase on the ground—as if she's trying to get the best running time.

Except, she can't, because she's not at a track and field competition. And her two new friends here clearly don't work out. The girl is struggling to keep up on her shorter legs and the guy is basically wheezing.

"We're almost there!" Duri tries to encourage them just like she does her teammates. "Just a little more."

She doesn't look back to see the other two teens' reactions, though. She can finally see the entrance to the ride. Duri grips tighter to the hands she's holding despite the guy's hand being sweaty and the girl's feeling like a dead fish.

Duri mentally counts out the seconds. 3. 2. 1. And the group bursts out into the sunlight.

No longer below overhead fans, a humid heat wave smacks Duri in the face, causing even more sweat to drip down her temples. As she catches her breath, her senses take in the change of scenery.

No more generic adventurous music from hidden speakers or people chatting in line. Out here, Bon Jovi's "It's My Life" plays from speakers sitting at the base of the palm trees lining the sidewalk. Happy screams mix with the clacking sound Duri associates with roller coasters. A couple of kids run past her, shouting and laughing, as a pair of elderly adults yell at them to slow down.

As Duri looks around at the food stands, merchandise stores, and other rides, trying to figure out where to go, she feels the prickling sensation of being watched. The ride attendants at the entrance look at the three teens quizzically. People joining the line look too.

Duri doesn't want to draw even more attention, so she lets go of the two hands she's been holding. After wiping sweat from her forehead with her wrist, she offers a fake smile to anyone looking their way. Then she motions for her companions to follow her, but doesn't check to see if they do.

Duri reaches the Galactic Survival gift shop that the ride exits into. By the time she goes inside, her adrenaline has gone down. Her heart rate slows almost back to normal and her breathing evens out. Trying to finish calming her nerves, she inhales the scent of new merchandise, sunscreen, and stuffy yet somehow also cool air.

After a few moments, Duri feels safe enough among the shopping crowd, oblivious to the drama that happened in line, to turn around and face her little group. The guy is leaning against the wall between displays, struggling to catch his breath. The girl is watching him with concern as she stands in the middle of the row Duri chose.

They're surrounded by shoppers trying to find their sizes. T-shirts line the wall, designed with the Galactic Survival ships, colorful galaxy patterns, and corny sayings like, "Try surviving my galaxy". It's the second busiest part of the store, aside from the toy section.

But Duri doesn't want to be around kids. She's in too bad a mood to watch her language.

"Can you believe that bastard?!" Duri exclaims as she gestures vaguely back in the ride's direction. But it doesn't seem like either of the other two hear her.

The other girl asks the guy, "Are you okay?"

He nods and waves her off before reaching into his pocket to pull out an inhaler. After taking two puffs, he lets out a deep breath and puts the inhaler away again. Duri mentally kicks herself.

Of course, he has asthma.

She should've been able to tell by the way he'd been wheezing. There's a difference between struggling to catch your breath because you're out of shape and struggling to breathe because your lungs don't work like they're supposed to. Duri knows that. She has a teammate with asthma.

"Shit, I'm sorry, man," Duri apologizes. "Feeling better?"

He glares at her for a second. In the sunlight from the store entrance and the overhead fluorescent lights, Duri can see he has deep green eyes. His gaze softens as he shakes his head.

"I'm fine."

"Are you sure?" The other girl tilts her head. "Your words say one thing, but your actions say another."

As he catches his breath, he shakes his head again, then nods, and then shakes his head a third time.

"Kind of getting mixed signals here, dude," Duri says. The guy points at her.

"That's what I was shaking my head at."

Duri's thin eyebrows meet in the middle. "What?"

He rolls his eyes, but smirks. "I should probably be clearer, huh?"

"That *would* be beneficial," says the other girl.

He nods and straightens up. Using the palm of one of his hands, he makes sure his afro is still in good shape.

Now that he's calmed down, he explains, "I'm nonbinary. Well, actually gender fluid."

"Ah, okay," Duri says in understanding. She raises both hands up. "Say no more. Sorry about that."

"Uh, can you please say more, actually?" asks the other girl.

When Duri and her new gender fluid friend both look at her, she bites her lower lip nervously. Or maybe excitedly? It's difficult for Duri to tell.

"No problem. When my dads adopted me, they were told I was a boy, so they named me Alexander. But I realized I sometimes feel like Alexandra. And sometimes I'm just Alex, like today. Right now, I'm going by they/them pronouns."

They gesture towards their outfit as if that explains everything.

Duri takes in Alex's style. The light pink color of their pants and their purple shoes. The thin long-sleeved brown shirt that hugs their every muscle. They have a small flower shaped ring in their pointed nose too.

They're wearing a little blush, showing off their cheekbones over their clean-shaven jaw. They're also wearing brown lipstick, black mascara and eyeliner, and glittery bluish-purple eyeshadow.

After looking at Alex's eyes, Duri finally notices that their white glasses don't have any lenses. She should've noticed when the glasses didn't steam up with the exercise.

"Hi Alex," Duri replies. "I'm Duri. I'm just cis and go by she/her."

Alex gives her a genuine smile now. "Nice to meet you, Duri."

"Well, I'm Jaya. And I guess I also go by she/her. Though I don't know what cis means."

"Cisgender," Duri and Alex both say.

Duri looks at Alex to explain, but they gesture for her to go on. "That just means I identify my gender with the biological sex I was born with."

"Or assigned at birth," Alex adds. Duri nods in agreement.

"How do you know so much about this?"

Jaya aimed her question at Duri, who expected it. She appreciates that Jaya's questioning is curious, not accusatory.

"My school has a Genders and Sexualities Alliance group that I go to sometimes. I'm bi."

"Ah, so you're one of us," Alex says as they push off the wall. They wink at Duri. She's glad to see they feel better.

Duri expects Jaya to continue to appear uncomfortable. Instead, Jaya's shoulders relax.

"Sorry for all the questions. I'm just used to being the only queer one, you know? I'm asexual. And though I've read up on sexual orientation, I've done little research on gender identities."

Jaya tucks a strand of hair behind her ear self-consciously. But neither Alex nor Duri seem phased by the admission of guilt.

Alex actually appears to be just as surprised about Jaya's sexual identity as Duri is. At least, if their facial expression is any sign. Duri assumes it's because, with all of Jaya's questioning, she appeared to be more like a non-queer person trying to understand.

Not that Duri can blame her. Duri acted the same when she first came out.

"I get it," Alex replies. "I'm the only openly queer person at my school."

"Really?" Jaya perks up. "Where do you go?"

Alex winces. "Son of God Christian Prep."

"Ugh," Duri replies.

She knows that private school. It's where that dick Ben attends. Understanding clicks then and Duri adds, "So that's how you know him."

Alex seems to know exactly who Duri's referring to. They fidget with their nose ring.

"He's kind of my ex-boyfriend."

Duri grimaces. "Well, shit."

"Uh," Jaya interjects, nervously scratching her upturned nose. "Not to keep asking questions, but..."

Alex laughs, a light sound that Duri finds comforting. "Of course, hun."

Chapter 5: Alex

ALEX AND THE GIRLS find a somewhat emptier corner of the store to sit on the gray-tiled floor. After being in line for half an hour, running, and standing around talking, all three teens want to get off their feet. Alex worries a store employee will say something, but no one seems to care.

"I used to date the guy that we almost got paired with for the ride," Alex begins, glad their breathing is back to normal. They try not to think about how Ben used to take their breath away. Faster than asthma ever could. Literally.

Alex learned quickly that they needed to keep their inhaler on the nightstand whenever Ben came over.

At Alex's words, Jaya's glossy lips drop into a small O shape. A moment passes before she closes her jaw with a little clack of her teeth.

"What are the odds, right?" Duri chimes in as she props up one of her legs and rests her arms on her knee.

"Not good," Alex replies. "This is Ben's favorite ride." They lean their head back against the navy blue wall, their hair a nice cushion. As they continue speaking, their eyes trail over the fake planets hanging from the ceiling, imitating the solar system. "But I thought this was a safe time because of church."

Duri gestures excitedly towards Alex.

"Right?!" She lets out a groan. "I totally forgot there's a guest preacher today. It's Pastor Caleb's anniversary with his wife."

"And they're celebrating with their son in an amusement park?" asks Jaya in dismay.

Alex and Duri nod emphatically.

"I can't tell you how many times I talked to Ben about being too close with his parents," Alex explains. "It's kind of weird."

"Yeah," Duri adds. "I swear Rebecca would chew his food for him if she could."

Alex can't help but laugh at Duri's comment, which elicits a laugh out of her, too. Even Jaya is grinning.

"Anyway," they continue, "we broke up a few weeks ago. Apparently I was,"—Alex does air quotes with their index and middle fingers for the next part—"'ruining his high school senior year experience.'"

"Douchebag," Duri responds in solidarity.

Jaya bites her lower lip before commenting, "That's so mean."

Alex tries to clarify, struggling not to sound defensive. "Ben's not out of the closet. Obviously."

They direct this last word towards Duri. She's the only other person here who knows anything about their ex. She gives one head nod in response.

Alex continues, "We've been dating in secret ever since he asked me out at the beginning of the school year."

It occurs to Alex that maybe they're getting close to TMI territory, but they don't really mind. It's nice to talk to someone outside of their dads about what happened with Ben.

"So, I guess that got to him because it's not like he could take me to his friends' parties or his chess tournaments." Alex swallows hard before adding, "Or prom."

That last one still stings. Alex feels stupid when they think about how hopeful they'd been for months, dreaming about a promposal from their boyfriend. They try to reassure themselves that it seemed plausible.

After all, Ben was romantic in private, always whispering sweet nothings and everythings in Alex's ear. And he was considerate of Alex's feelings, always willing to hold them as they processed their thoughts out loud.

He even seemed supportive when Alex talked about Hanukkah and Kwanzaa. Or when Alex talked about the unique identity they've created as a black person adopted by two white men.

Ben seemed to care about everything.

So, Alex had high hopes for Ben when prom season came around. They imagined opening their locker one day to find dozens of tiny paper hearts taped to the inside of the locker door, spelling out the question.

Or maybe Ben would give Alex a ride home. He sometimes did that when he could wait after school for Alex to get out of Mathletes. And on the passenger seat? A handwritten card with the question.

Or maybe Ben would ask Alex to meet in the empty classroom. The one they usually went to whenever Ben could get away from his friends at lunch. And Alex would find a picnic blanket on the floor. Bottles of bubbly cider. Delicious chocolate rugelach from the kosher bakery across the street.

And when Alex sat down, Ben would take their hands into his, make lingering eye contact, and ask the question:

"Will you go to prom with me?"

Clearly, Alex had way too long to daydream. Especially since the promposal never came.

Instead, Ben avoided the subject like one of those deadly space diseases in those sci-fi shows he likes so much.

And on prom night, Alex put on the new liquid eyeliner they recently learned how to wear, along with sparkling silver eyeshadow, eyelash extensions, and a kissable red lipstick and liner. Not to mention the perfect shade of foundation to hide any blemishes on their complexion, as well as glitter-infused blush to really highlight their cheekbones. To top it all off, they added several gemstone hair pins in their jet black afro.

That night, Alex put on the ironed white dress shirt they recently got for a cousin's bar mitzvah. They dressed up in the tux that their pops wore for his wedding with their dad. The tux they spent hours changing the fabric on the lapels for re-purposed silk in different shades of silver. It paired well with their silver high heels and eyeshadow.

For Ben's sake, Alex wanted to match the cheesy "Night Under the Stars" theme. So they also put on the star-shaped cufflinks they spent several nights thrifting online to find in good enough condition. They even put on a moon shaped nose ring—made from recycled sterling silver—for the occasion.

Last but not least, Alex added a few rhinestones to the tux's lapels. They hoped to draw Ben's attention when all the gems, silver, and glitter caught the light as Alex danced. Like swirling stardust sparkling in the night sky.

It was the best Alex could do considering the cisnormative dress code restrictions in place. "Girls" could only wear dresses or a skirt and blouse, while the "boys" could only wear suits, tuxes, or dress pants with a dress shirt.

Alex found this kind of thinking outdated, offensive, and limiting. Their creativity felt stifled, like a large bird in a small cage. They wanted to let their creativity soar! But they could only do that on their tablet.

At least Alex could add the modified A-line and trumpet prom dress designs they came up with to their portfolio. Even if they never got to make or wear them.

Despite all that, Alex still tried to make the most of the night. They went to prom with a group of friends and had a decent enough time. But they couldn't help looking over their shoulder every chance they got to check out their boyfriend.

Ben looked so handsome in his simple black suit, showing off his broad shoulders and adorable butt. He had gelled his hair back, something he hated to do, but occasionally did for Alex because he knew the hairstyle made his partner swoon. Alex still hopes Ben did that for them.

He wore a silver tie too. But Alex never found out if Ben meant to match their color scheme. Not that it matters anymore.

"Oh well," Alex says now after realizing the girls were waiting for them to continue. "Maybe he was right. I knew what I was signing up for, but he probably didn't. It's not like he ever dated anyone before, let alone someone queer. I never dated before either, but at least I've been out since freshman year. Maybe it was my responsibility to initiate him or something."

And as Alex says this, it's the first time they actually fear Ben was right.

Chapter 6: Jaya

"ARE YOU FUCKING *kidding* me right now?" Duri exclaims, causing Jaya to jump a little. Duri doesn't seem to notice, though, as she rants, "This idiot asks *you* out, then *blames* you for not dating publicly even though *he* kept *you* a secret. Then he dumps you a month before graduation, and you think *he's* right?"

When Duri pauses, Jaya thinks it's so Alex has a chance to respond. But Duri just shakes her head vehemently.

"Uh-uh. Nope. Not happening." Duri scoffs and then mutters, "Just like the little dipshit. Not taking accountability for his own actions."

Alex gazes at Duri until she puts out her hands, palms facing up, in a "What?" kind of gesture.

"I've just never had someone so... on my side before," Alex says. "I mean, aside from my dads, that is."

"You don't have supportive friends at school?" Jaya asks.

"No, I do," Alex replies. "They just don't get the queer thing. You know?"

Jaya nods. She knows. She doesn't go to a private school because her single mom can't afford it. But she goes to a charter school where only a few students are out. So no one's started a GSA and she's too anxious to change that.

She has friends, sure, but sexuality rarely comes up. A couple of her friends are from the school newspaper, where Jaya is a Junior Editor. But they don't really spend time together outside of that, so they mainly talk about school news and article revisions.

Most of Jaya's friends are fellow bookworms from the student-run book club. They read across a wide variety of genres such as fantasy (her favorite), horror, romance, non-fiction, and more. But even though the amount of ethnic and racial diversity has grown in their chosen books—which she appreciates considering she's Indian, specifically a Kannadiga, on her mom's side—Jaya has yet to come across an ace character like her.

"I feel for you two," Duri says with a sympathetic smile. "I'm the only openly queer person on my track and field team, but there are a lot at my school. Maybe it's because I go to a public school. I don't know."

"That must be nice," Jaya replies.

Duri scrunches up her nose. "Yeah, but I don't really hang out with anyone from the GSA outside of meetings. That *is* how I met my girlfriend, though. And our relationship is *not* a secret."

"As it should be," Alex says adamantly.

Nodding, she continues, "My girl's actually ace like you." Duri knocks the toe of her light pink sneaker against one of Jaya's black buckle shoes.

Jaya perks up at this, ignoring the fact that Duri may have scuffed up one of her favorite pair of shoes. These shoes probably weren't the best decision for an amusement park, anyway.

"Really? What's she like?"

Duri's eyes flick towards Alex. "I don't want to take Alex's moment here. We're supporting them right now." Alex waves a hand of encouragement.

"Please. I'd love to hear about a healthy queer relationship."

Duri clearly tries to fight a smile, but she apparently can't help it as her dimples appear. Her cheeks redden as she speaks.

"Well, she's the most amazing girl I know. She's bubbly and outgoing. Funny and so smart. Romantic, sweet, and supportive. Oh! And a *gah-reat* kisser." Duri laughs as she runs a self-conscious hand through her short hair. "Wanna see a pic?"

"Obviously!" Alex exclaims at the same time that Jaya says, "Of course."

Duri fishes out her phone from her jean pocket and turns it towards the other teenagers. The phone's home screen shows Duri and a girl with honey colored skin, a spiked brown pixie cut with blonde highlights, and full lips.

In the picture, she has an arm around Duri's waist, pulling her close. Duri has an arm around the girl's shoulders, the other arm apparently reaching out to hold the phone. Duri's planting a big kiss on her girlfriend's cheek, who has her eyes closed at the show of affection.

"Aw!" Alex says with a squeal. "You two look so happy together."

Duri gazes wistfully at the phone before putting it away. "Yeah, we are. Thanks."

"What's her name?" Jaya asks.

She's becoming conscious of how many questions she's asking. How she's prying into the lives of these two, basically strangers, she just met today. But both seem so ready to open up their hearts, as desperate for connection as Jaya.

Just as emotionally raw.

"Mariana," Duri replies. "Or Marí for short."

The three of them are silent for a moment. No one knows what to say until Alex looks at Jaya.

"What about you, hun?"

She blinks rapidly as Duri turns towards her as well. Jaya points an index finger at her own ample chest.

"Me? Oh, I'm too anxious to date." She scratches her head for a moment. Then she adds, "I actually might be aromantic, too. I'm not sure. Still figuring this stuff out?"

Jaya plans to let someone else take the floor. She usually does that when the spotlight is on her for too long. Instead, she pushes herself a bit more out of her comfort zone. She feels like it's only fair, considering how much her acquaintances have shared so far.

Or maybe it's *because* Alex and Duri are only acquaintances that it's easier for Jaya to speak her mind. After all, neither Alex nor Duri have any preconceived notions about Jaya. She doesn't have to worry about being the perfect daughter or responsible big sister. She doesn't have to fit in just one box—newspaper editor *or* bookworm—like she does with her friends from school.

Jaya can just be Jaya.

"Actually," she says, "I'm thinking about using my writing as an opportunity to explore that. My romantic orientation, I mean..."

She lets her voice trail off, unsure how anyone's going to react. She expects someone to call her a dork, like her little brother does when she talks about her writing to him. But she gets a positive response.

"That's cool," Duri responds kindly.

"Mhm," Alex agrees. "What do you like to write?"

Jaya sits up at the invitation.

"Fantasy! I love the whole idea of magic and possibilities. The beautiful world-building and medieval time periods. Although, Urban Fantasy has been a thing for a while. Like *The Mortal Instruments* series by Cassandra Clare. I enjoy it, but not as much as, say, classics like *The Chronicles of Narnia* series by C. S. Lewis. Though Urban Fantasy has better ethnic diversity. I've been meaning to read Kalynn Bayron's *This Poison Heart* series. You can probably see the trend of series here. I love series. It's so much easier to find my next book that way, you know? Takes off some of the pressure. There's so much to read. So little time."

She lets out a nervous laugh as she forces herself to shut up. She can't believe she's blabbered on for so long. That's something she can only do with her bookish friends. Her mom and brother always interrupt her when she gets on one of her book related rants. To Jaya's surprise, though, Duri ends up laughing too.

"If you had told me that all we had to do to get you to *really* talk was bring up books, I would've done that already."

Alex laughs too. "Right? I love how passionate you are about books! That's me with sustainable fashion. Don't get me *started* on how wasteful the clothing industry is." They shudder. "But you can follow me @EcoFashionByDanieli on TikTok if you ever *actually* want to hear one of those rants. Or see my eco-friendly designs."

"I'm on TikTok too," Duri says. "@SeongDuri, but I post random crap."

Alex shrugs one shoulder. "I'll take all the followers I can get. What about you, Jaya?"

Jaya excitingly takes out her phone from her dress pocket. God, she loves dresses with pockets. They're so rare.

"Sure! @JayaFosterReads. I'm mainly on there for BookTok, though. I don't really post anything but book recs."

"That's okay," Alex says. They take out their phone at the same time as Duri.

"Alex," Duri says, scrolling on her phone. "You're really talented."

"Oh, stop it, keep going," Alex says with a wave of their hand. The girls laugh.

Jaya doesn't know anything about fashion. But she can tell by the amount of content on Alex's profile that they've worked hard on these designs. And she's not the only one who thinks so, considering Alex has about 3,000 followers.

Duri's profile is just shy of 1,000. And her profile does indeed have a bunch of random different videos. So many that Jaya doesn't have time to figure out what kinds.

Jaya hopes no one says anything about the fact that she's still below five hundred followers.

There's a short, awkward pause after the three follow one another. Jaya realizes none of them had said anything before about staying in touch. She wonders if she should say something. But before she can, Alex returns to the previous conversation.

"Anyway," they say, putting their phone back in their pocket. "I'm actually going to Pratt Institute in New York next fall for Fashion Design."

"Congrats!" Duri says as she puts her phone away as well. "It's pretty cool that you've found your thing, Alex."

"That's amazing." Jaya plays with her phone in her lap as Alex's words fully register in her mind. She asks, "And your parents are okay with that?"

She tries not to let her eagerness show, but she yearns for advice on how to get parents on board with a career path they wouldn't choose themselves.

Alex fidgets with their nose ring. "They're not ecstatic about it, but they support me. Dad is a lawyer and Pops owns a successful accounting firm. So they'd rather I choose a career that's more stable and not so competitive. But they want to see me happy."

Jaya lets Alex's last sentence sink in. She imagines what her mom would say if Jaya tried to use that as an argument to study English as a major in college.

"*I want you to be happy,* chinna. *But you know what will make you the happiest? Having a reliable, well-paying job so you don't have to worry about making rent.*"

Chapter 7: Duri

"LET ME GUESS," DURI says, "you also already have your life figured out."

Jaya puts a hand to her cheek, though Duri isn't sure if she's hiding a smile or a grimace.

"Well," Jaya replies, "I may have gotten into a really good writing program to study English in college."

"What?!" Alex exclaims. "Where?"

Jaya visibly swallows, her chest seeming to rise faster before she speaks. Duri hopes she doesn't have another asthmatic on her hands.

Before she can ask, Jaya replies, "Dartmouth? I got a full ride because of my grades and SAT scores. And my extracurriculars. And because my mom doesn't make that much money. As a social worker, you know..."

Great. Another ivy league school. Just like Hana.

Alex pumps a fist in the air. "Yes! You're going to be in Massachusetts. That's super close to New York!" They gasp. "We could hang out." They cover their mouth with one of their hands like they can't even believe what they just said. After a moment, they clear their throat. "I mean, if you'd like to stay in touch. I hope"—their green eyes flicker to Duri—"that both of you want to stay in touch." Alex smiles and adds, "We *are* friends on TikTok now."

Duri struggles to respond. She can't stop thinking about the fact that her twin sister is going to be at some New England college near her two new friends. At least Marí is staying local, going to the University of Central Florida to study Child Psychology.

But still. Damn. Like, WTF?

Jaya beams back at Alex. "I'd love that."

She reaches towards Alex, hesitates, then grabs their hand for a brief squeeze. She smiles at Duri too. It's then that Duri realizes Alex is waiting for a response from her. She knows she's being selfish. She should be supportive of Jaya opening up, but Duri doesn't know what to say.

It's rare, but it happens. So she just nods.

She doesn't need to say anything, though. Soon enough, Alex gets Jaya talking about her writing again. Jaya explains some story idea she has about a book series where the main character is an asexual, and potentially aromantic, mermaid.

And Duri can't help but tune out. It's not because of the chosen topic, though. She *does* enjoy the occasional audiobook here and there.

No, Duri's thinking about the screaming match she got into with her sister last night. Last week's argument too. Also, the fight from a few weeks before that. And the time they almost got physical months ago. When Hana found out she was accepted into Harvard, and then learned Duri only applied to one college. A community college.

Duri thought their parents would be the ones on her case. They used to be when she was younger. Constantly comparing her faults to her "older" sister's achievements.

Hana walked first. Hana talked first. She was potty trained first. She got into the honors program. Her part-time job as a restaurant hostess will look much better on her college applications than Duri's unemployed ass. When was Duri going to catch up to the example her "big" sister set for her?

Okay. To be fair, Duri's parents never called her an ass. But she felt like one.

Duri's parents went with her to so many parent-teacher meetings. And every teacher said the same thing. Duri's incredibly intelligent, but lazy. She's creative, but daydreams too much. Though she participates in class, she doesn't test well. She just needs to apply herself. Keep herself motivated.

Blah blah.

Somewhere along the way, Duri's parents seemed to stop caring. It was barely noticeable when it started. One less lecture. One more thing Duri got away with. But eventually it's like they just gave up on her. And she still doesn't know why.

What was the last straw? Her SAT scores? Did she say something wrong? She's been pretty sassy to her sister, but she always tries to at least be respectful about how she speaks to their parents.

Whatever.

Duri's gotten by just fine with a C average and her parents seem glad enough that she's passing her classes. They never even say anything about her bisexuality either, though they don't understand it and probably secretly think she's going to hell.

But Hana? She's their pride and joy, their bright hope, the bearer of their future grandchildren and shit. And did Hana think that was enough? No.

Hana took over the role their parents should have. Constantly berating Duri to stop wasting time and do her homework. To grow up already and apply to a *real* college. To get her shit together and just pick a major.

And Duri would just hurl insults back:

"Go do yourself, bitch." "Apply my foot up your ass, why don't you?" "Oh, just pick a dick to suck on."

And every time Duri felt guilt compress her stomach into a ball that she could dribble down a court and dunk to win the World's Worst Sister award.

Duri doesn't believe that being queer or swearing are sins. God has better things to do than care about who Duri loves, or what she says to herself. If anything is a sin, though, it's the way she treats her sister.

But Hana just doesn't get it! She doesn't understand that Duri already tells herself all the same things that Hana tells her. Duri already tries to force herself to get her damn life together, but she can't. No matter how hard she tries.

And the amount of anxiety that brings? Every time she fails?

It's what drove her to join the track and field team. Because running makes her already racing heart make sense. And running is something she excels at. Running a competition. Running from her responsibilities.

What's the difference, anyway?

"Duri?" Jaya asks.

"Hey," Alex joins in a soothing voice. "What's up?"

Duri drags herself back to the present, trying to ground herself by focusing on the concern on her new friends' faces.

"Sorry."

"That's okay," Jaya replies.

"There's nothing to be sorry about," Alex says. "What's on your mind?"

Duri gives Alex a soft smile, touched by their concern. Then she looks at Jaya, who's patiently waiting. Duri sighs.

"You both know what you want to do in college. That's great! But I haven't figured it out yet."

"Ah," Alex responds in understanding.

"Oh," Jaya says soon after. "If you don't mind my asking, do you... *want* to go to college?"

Duri scrunches up her nose. "I guess? I'm going to Valencia in the fall. Hoping I can knock out my gen eds, get my AA, and hopefully figure out what I want to do by then so I can transfer and join Marí at UCF."

Duri hopes neither of them will say anything about how unrealistic it is to believe she'll still be with her high school sweetheart by then. Hana would totally throw that back in Duri's face if she knew. But Duri doesn't want to go to UCF just because of Marí. It's a good school. And they have a direct transfer program with Valencia Community College.

Marí going there is just a bonus.

A sexy bonus.

Instead of any pushback, though, Alex says, "That's a solid plan."

"Yes, it's really not that bad," Jaya replies, almost like she's saying it to herself. "Do you not get good grades or something?"

Duri tries not to roll her eyes. "No, I don't." She sighs and adds, "Not that I don't try."

She tries not to think about how close she was to repeating her sophomore year. If her parents hadn't paid for tutoring, she would've graduated one year after Hana.

Duri passed, but barely.

"That's unfortunate," Jaya says softly.

Duri hopes the conversation will go in a different direction, but Alex pries on.

"Wait, what do you mean by that?"

"What do you mean, what do I mean?"

Uh-oh. Duri's feeling the heat in her cheeks. The clawing anxiety grabbing at her chest. Alex has clearly struck a nerve and Duri doesn't know how to un-strike it.

"I *mean* that I've sat down to study a bajillion times, but constantly can't stop myself from getting distracted by videos online or playing games on my phone. I *mean* that even the few times I *do* somehow study, which is so rare that it's a freaking miracle, I can't focus on tests or quizzes. Too busy paying attention to the beat of my classmate's pen tapping on the desk, or I just watch the clock tick for way too long. Next thing I know, I'm out of time!

"Or like in English—no offense, Jaya—when I have to write an essay. I start with a thesis, but I can't help going down rabbit holes in my research. And then my essay ends up being too short because I researched so much I procrastinated writing or it's too long because I ramble on for pages. So, *that's* what I mean."

Breathing heavily, Duri literally bites her tongue. Frustrated, unshed tears spring to her eyes. But like hell if she's going to cry in front of her new friends. Either Alex and Jaya can tell and they want to give Duri a moment to compose herself or they're too stunned to reply.

The three teens sit in noisy silence for a few moments, saying nothing to each other, while park guests and store employees chatter in the background and Aqua's "Lollipop (Candyman)" plays from the speakers overhead.

Finally, to Duri's surprise, Jaya is the one to break the silence.

"It sounds like you might have ADHD." Pause. "Uh, have you ever, like, considered that?"

Chapter 8: Jaya

JAYA FIGHTS THE URGE to cover her mouth with both her hands. She can't believe she just blurted out a diagnosis to someone. What is she, a therapist? She knows nothing about mental health or learning disabilities!

Except she does a little, doesn't she?

She'd be kidding herself if she didn't admit that Duri's stressful confession sounded just like what Karib goes through. Jaya can't even remember how many times she's stayed home with him so their mom can have a parent-teacher conference.

It used to annoy Jaya because she can't read when she's babysitting. Even if he didn't have Attention Deficit Hyperactivity Disorder, Karib is still a young boy. And all young boys are energetic, getting bored easily with the same video games.

And they eat. A lot.

Jaya also knows if she doesn't help right now, she'll regret it later. She's never been able to see someone in need without offering her assistance. If it's in her power, at least.

Sometimes, she can go too far. Doing things for the other person as if that's the best solution. Like when she thought she had to impress a boy in middle school because one of her friends thought they'd make a cute couple. Jaya did his English homework for a week before they almost got caught. That scared Jaya enough to stop.

Jaya waits now for Duri to say something, but she merely stares back. Or rather, it's almost like she's looking through Jaya.

After a beat, Duri lets out a resolute, "Huh."

Alex crosses their legs in a pretzel position, leans an elbow on one of their knees, and then props their head on the palm of their hand. They, too, look pensive, as if trying to confirm Jaya's theory in their mind.

"You should look into that," Alex says. "Can't hurt, right?"

Jaya lets out a breath she didn't even realize she'd been holding. Relief sweeps through her as Duri nods slowly, appearing to relax into the idea. Duri's shoulders, which Jaya notices had been by her ears, lower to a more comfortable position. Jaya takes the opportunity to step tentatively into the next part of her idea.

"Maybe you can see a counselor or someone about that when you start school. Or over the summer? Because my brother has ADHD and his teachers give him accommodations that really help. Like, let me think, uh, longer times on tests and quizzes and... he's allowed to take them in another classroom in order to focus too and... oh! He gets extensions on longer assignments. That's it. I can't really remember. My mom would know?"

Jaya forces herself to stop talking. Her nervous rambling has always been one of her most annoying habits, though she knows she's probably harder on herself about it than other people. Her friends and family actually care enough about her that they don't seem to mind.

Unless it's about books and she's talking to her mom or brother. They'll stop her then.

Actually, Karib just spaces out whenever she talks about anything other than *Lego Star Wars*. Or whatever video game, show, or movie he's into at the time.

Preteen boys. Sigh.

"Thanks, Jay," Duri says, much to Jaya's surprise. They haven't even known each other a full day, and she's already getting called by her nickname? She has to admit she finds that sweet. Duri continues, "You may be onto something, you gorgeous example of humanity you."

At first, Jaya just blinks a few times, unsure how to respond to Duri's elaborate compliment.

In the end, she simply replies with a "Thank... you?"

Alex bursts out in a fit of giggles, which unlocks something within Jaya. She allows herself to laugh along, fully and completely, with no inhibitions. She leans forward as she does so, accidentally pressing into her phone, which she now realizes is still on her lap.

Jaya jolts back up, almost hitting her head against the wall, which just makes her laugh harder. Duri joins in on the laughter. Soon enough, the three of them are struggling to catch their breath. Alex puts a stop to it first, waving their inhaler around.

"Don't make me use this again! Please!"

"Okay, okay," Duri says, calming down as she leans back on her hands. Jaya also tries to get her laughter under control.

The three let out a collective sigh. Then Duri places a hand on Alex's forearm.

"Hey, sorry I snapped at you. You hit a sore spot, but that wasn't your fault."

"Don't worry your pretty little head about it," Alex replies with a squeeze of Duri's hand. Then Alex brushes her hand off, shimmies their shoulders, and looks at Jaya. "Enough sentimentality. I'm not wearing waterproof mascara."

Duri rolls her eyes, but smirks. "Okay..." she replies in a singsong voice.

"So, *Jay*," Alex says, emphasizing Jaya's nickname as if taking it out for a test drive. "I don't think you finished telling us about your writing. Congratulations on getting into Dartmouth. That's huge!"

"Oh, yeah!" Duri chimes in. "Same, congrats!"

Heat crawls up Jaya's neck, contrasting against the air-conditioned atmosphere in the store. She focuses on stretching out her cramping legs, much to her muscles' relief, before replying.

"Thanks."

"So, what's the problem?" Duri asks. "A full ride to an ivy seems great, if you ask me."

"I know," Jaya responds, reminding herself that Duri's bluntness is just part of her personality. "The issue is that my mom doesn't know."

Growing up with a single parent, Jaya has always been super close to her mom. They always had a special bond. Jaya is not sure if it's because they're both girls or because she was older than Karib when their parents divorced, but she used to tell her mom everything.

But now? That's changing. And it's uncomfortable. She doesn't know how to do anything her mom doesn't approve of...

"There it is," Alex replies to Jaya's admission, though it takes a second to recall it's not her inward one. "Our girl's going off to a famous college, up the East coast, *on her own*, to follow her dream to become the next Jane Austen. And there's nothing her mom can do because she doesn't know!"

Jaya wonders briefly why being on her own isn't what's worrying her the most. Maybe it's because she's always kept well to herself. It's being on her own *against her mom's wishes* that's scarier.

"I don't think Jane Austen wrote fantasy," Duri responds, completely bypassing the rest of Alex's commentary on Jaya's plans.

"She didn't? Oh, well. I don't read that much. I mean, I like fashion magazines. *Vanity Fair* is my favorite. And I enjoy memoirs. I guess you could say non-fiction is more my style."

"Okay, but come on," Duri replies. "You saw the movies, right? Marí's obsessed with *Pride and Prejudice*, though I prefer *Pride and Prejudice and Zombies*." She pauses for a second. Then she adds, "But that last one doesn't really count for anything."

"True. Have you seen—Oh!" Alex cuts themselves off, shaking their head. It's as if they finally noticed that Jaya has just been watching the conversation volley back and forth between her new friends like a ping-pong match. "I totally derailed us, didn't I?"

Jaya shrugs a little, not really minding. She wants to know what Alex was about to ask.

But then Duri's blushing and sending an apologetic glance in Jaya's direction.

"Same. Sorry."

"Continue, hun," Alex says.

They tap Jaya's knee, which is barely covered by the end of her dress. It's a fleeting touch, like a butterfly landing on a flower. She doesn't mind it.

"It's fine," Jaya says with a small smile. "I rather enjoyed that."

Forgetting the lighthearted conversation about movies, and recalling the original topic they left off on, Jaya's smile drops.

She clears her throat and continues, "So, it's not just that I haven't, like, told my mom that I got into Dartmouth. I haven't even told her that I plan to major in English. Or that I want to be a writer. Like professionally. She knows I write, but she thinks it's just a hobby."

Alex makes a sucking noise through their teeth. "I've been there."

"Ouch," Duri replies. "That sucks. I guess that's the silver lining of my problem. Can't hide my dreams when I don't know what they are yet." She elbows Alex playfully, who rolls their eyes.

"Don't be self-deprecating, darling. It's not a good look on you. Doesn't match your complexion."

Duri laughs and blows Alex a kiss. They pretend to catch it and save it in their pocket for later.

Jaya's heart swells in her chest at the tenderness of it all. These moments of vulnerability they've been able to achieve the same day they met. Something she's struggled with people she's known for years.

She thinks of how excited her mom was when Jaya received her first college acceptance. But she couldn't bring herself to admit to her mom that it was a safety school.

She remembers all the times she opened her email, only to find yet another article sent by her mom with headlines like, "Top 10 Majors that Make the Most Money" or "How to Pick a Degree that Will Pay the Bills and Bring Peace of Mind" or "So You Haven't Picked a College? Try These 3 Tips to Plan Your Post-Secondary Future".

And on and on they went.

And Karib. He wants to help, but he's too young. Yes, he's in middle school, but he still doesn't know much about the world. Not that Jaya knows much more. However, she knows that "just pick the cheapest college, study the easiest program, and make a lot of money" isn't a plan.

At least, it's not a plan that would work for Jaya.

She still thanks Karib for his advice just the same, though. And, much to his annoyance, she always ends those conversations with a ruffle of his thick dirty blonde hair that's much like their dad's, as well as a, "Thanks, kid."

But Duri and Alex? Both of them *really* listen. They both respond with empathy. Help problem solve and encourage. It makes Jaya want to open up, valuing all the advice and feedback she can get.

And so she does.

Chapter 9: Alex

TAPPING A MANICURED nail against their chin, Alex thinks over Jaya's ordeal. They reflect on her questions again: How can she come clean to her mom without hurting her? And how can she convince her mom to let her go?

"Just rip off the bandage," Duri advises. "The longer you wait, the harder it's going to be." She scrunches up her nose. "I know about being anxious. And putting things off. Trust me." She reaches over and squeezes Jaya's calf lightly. "You'll feel better once it's out of there"—she points at Jaya's heart—"and it's out here." Duri gestures to the part of the store they'd been hanging out in earlier.

"Amongst the t-shirts?" Jaya asks coyly, much to Alex's surprise.

She's really gaining confidence as the conversation continues, and Alex likes it. It's a side of her that Alex and Duri can bring out that even seems to surprise Jaya, if her nervous expression after she speaks is any sign.

Jaya continues, "I'm fond of that one."

She points at the shirt that's on the closest mannequin. It reads, "My friend survived the Galactic Survival ride, and all I got was this lazy t-shirt."

Alex laughs dryly. "I'm impressed they got all that text on the front."

They turn away from the mannequin, not wanting to waste any of their knowledge about the dos and don'ts of fashion on shabby theme park merchandise. Like how the letters will fall in the wash. Or how the spacing between the letters is off. And not in an accidentally on purpose kind of way that's aesthetically pleasing.

And don't even get them *started* on the color palette. Neon gold letters on a neon chartreuse shirt? *And* on a neon orange mannequin, no less?

So cringey.

Shaking their head, Alex gets back to the original conversation at hand.

"I think Duri's right. Still, be careful with what you say. It helped my dads to know that I had a back-up plan in case my dream to start my own sustainable clothing brand doesn't pan out." Alex sighs. "I promised that I'd try marketing in that case."

"That's actually a great idea," Jaya says.

"Yes. I have them from time to time. Thank you very much."

The color seems to drain from Jaya's oval face as she blurts, "I didn't mean—! No! Like..."

Alex swats at Jaya playfully. "I'm just teasing. I know I've got brains *and* beauty."

She visibly relaxes and gives Alex a half-smile. "Yes, that is true." Alex dips their head in gratitude. Jaya continues, "I just can't believe I never thought of that sooner."

"What would you do?" Duri asks. "For your back-up plan."

Jaya thinks for a moment. "Technically, I could say the same as Alex. Content marketing is huge right now."

"Oh, yeah," Alex agrees.

They came across it in their research when presenting their idea of a back-up plan to their dads. If Alex can't make it big by designing clothes, they might as well help talk up other people's designs, right? They're no Shakespeare like Jaya, but Alex does all right. It's an option at least.

Still, if they needed to actually use their back-up plan, Alex plans on sticking to the graphic design part.

"That's not what I want to do, though," Jaya continues. She offers Alex an apologetic glance, which they dismiss with another wave of their hand. "If I'm not writing what I love to write, then I'd rather do something that inspires me to write."

"Aw, I love that!" Alex squeals, hands clasped at their chest. They can relate somewhat if they adapt the slogan.

If I'm not designing the fashion I want, then I'd rather do something that inspires others to design.

"And what would that be, then?" Duri asks, ignoring Alex.

Jaya chews on the inside of her cheek for a beat, then says, "Well, most authors teach writing at some point. Maybe I could be a middle school English teacher or something. I enjoy helping my little brother with his English homework. And I'm actually a tutor after school, too."

"That could work," Duri replies.

Jaya shrugs. "I guess. I can at least look into it. It's stable enough to appease my mom, even if it doesn't pay that well." She beams a smile in Alex's direction. "Thank you for the suggestion." Jaya turns the smile on Duri. "And the encouragement."

"No problem," Alex replies warmly.

"What are friends who just met for?" Duri replies before being silly and sticking out her tongue.

Jaya practically radiates ease and happiness as she settles back against the store wall. Barely a few seconds go by, though, before she's sitting rim rod straight.

"What?" Alex asks in concern.

"Do you see dead people?" Duri asks in a mock stage whisper.

Jaya ignores them both and just points at the store's entrance. "Isn't that what's his face?"

For a heartbeat, her question amuses Alex. They want to tease her about who she could possibly be referring to, but then they hear it. They hear that oh-so-familiar voice caressing their ears.

"Hey, Duri."

"FML," Duri mutters. Then she turns as Ben reaches the little group in the corner. In a mock cheery voice, she says, "Hey! How are you? I didn't know you were here!"

Alex wants to kick themselves in the butt right now. They'd gotten so caught up in the conversation with their new friends that they didn't realize how dumb it was to stay in such plain sight of the one person they were trying to avoid. Alex doesn't have to look at Duri to know that happened to her, too.

Ben doesn't look phased. "I literally just saw you in line less than two hours ago."

Despite being caught in her lie, Duri ignores his comment. "Yeah, about that. What took you so long?"

Ben sticks his thumb in the front pocket of his jeans, a suggestive gesture that he used to do for Alex's benefit. They have to swallow down their discomfort at the memories of shirts and pants finding the floor, intertwining limbs sliding against one another, and electric jolts at each point of skin-on-skin contact.

Completely oblivious to Alex's inner turmoil, Ben says, "My parents wanted to get something to eat. I left them getting coffee so I could see if y'all were still hanging out here. Like I saw when we got off the ride."

Alex swallows hard again. They'd been too focused on their group to notice Ben. How did that happen? Alex wasn't aware they were capable of that.

Jaya lets out a nervous squeak. Alex is sure she has a "deer in the headlights" look going on. But they can't bring themselves to tear their eyes off Ben.

Ben, who usually couldn't wear v-neck t-shirts like the one he's wearing now because of the hickeys Alex would leave on his collarbone. Whose blue eyes behind his glasses—*real* glasses—still remind Alex of the sky reflecting off the ocean's surface. Whose freckles appear to be sprinkled across his skin like water droplets on sand.

"Why?" Duri asks defensively. "What do you care?"

Ben rolls his eyes before his gaze lands on Alex. Their breath catches.

"Can we talk?"

Alex says nothing for a moment, completely taken aback by Ben's question. Jaya's the one who gets their attention, gently placing a hand on their shoulder like a hummingbird landing lightly on a tree branch.

"You don't have to if you don't want to," she whispers.

"Like hell they will," Duri mutters, but she quiets when Jaya gives her a stern look.

"It's fine," Alex says. They place a slightly shaky hand on the floor to help them get to their feet. "Thanks, girls. I'll be right back."

Alex doesn't look back as they lead Ben to the mannequin displays in front of the store. If they do, they'll see the worry on the girls' faces. Then Alex's frail bravado will crumble, causing them to crawl back into their friends' protective bubble. But they need to do this.

Whatever *this* is.

"So," Ben begins with a shy smile. His thin lips part to show the adorable little gap between his two front teeth.

"So," Alex replies, managing not to move any facial features.

Ben sticks his hands into the pockets of his shorts as he kicks the floor lightly with his sandal.

"Look," he says, "I just wanted to thank you."

Alex is so shocked that they almost literally step back. "Thank me? For what?"

Ben presses his lips together for a moment before explaining, "For hiding from my parents back there." He gestures with his chin towards where the ride exits into the store. "You know how my dad is. Even if he doesn't know that I'm..." His voice trails off before he continues, "anyway, he wouldn't even react well to me having friends who are..."

His voice trails off again as his eyes look Alex up and down. Like he's checking them out. Normally, this would thrill Alex. Stoke the flame of hope they had inside. But something different is simmering within the pit of their stomach.

Instead of melting at Ben's feet, Alex asks, "Friends, who are what?"

Ben swallows visibly. "You know."

Alex props a hand on one of their hips. "No, Ben, I don't know. Friends who are queer? Friends who are secretly in love with his son?"

"Shh!" Ben shushes loudly. He tries to look around inconspicuously, obviously wanting to make sure no one he knows heard Alex.

Duri's voice echoes in their mind. "Are you fucking *kidding* me right now?"

"Ridiculous." Alex doesn't realize they spoke out loud until Ben turns back abruptly.

"What's ridiculous?"

Alex sputters briefly before exclaiming, "You!" They gesture between themselves and Ben. "This!"

"Shh!" Ben shushes again, only this time he takes a step closer towards Alex. But they take a step back this time.

"Stop shushing me," Alex replies, although their voice is at a more normal level than they prefer.

"Okay, okay," Ben says softly, reaching to take Alex's hand like he's done so many times before. When Alex flinches, Ben lets his hand drop to his side. "I'm sorry. It's just... you know, I can't risk anyone finding out about us. *Ever*. I'm a worship leader at church, for goodness' sake."

"Of *course* I know that," Alex replies through gritted teeth.

"And I'm a PK," Ben continues, ignoring Alex. "Can you imagine how the congregation would react if they found out I'm..." Ben lets his voice trail off again, shaking his head. "You wouldn't want me to embarrass my dad like that, right?"

Alex takes in a shaky breath through their nose before letting it out in a huff.

"I get that being a Pastor's Kid is a lot."

Ben nods enthusiastically, clearly grateful Alex understands.

"But that doesn't mean you can treat me like... like..." Alex's throat catches and they take a moment to speak again. "Like I'm the root of all your problems."

Ben's eyes soften behind his lenses. "Babe," he begins in a soothing tone.

"Don't *babe* me," Alex snaps. "You lost the right to do that when you broke up with me."

"But—" Ben starts before Alex cuts him off.

"You know what? If you're going to act like we're still together, then *I'm* breaking up with *you*."

Ben's lips part in surprise. He mouths seemingly random syllables as he struggles to reply. Finally, he lands on the genius and well thought out conclusion of "Huh?"

Alex lets out a breathy laugh, the simmering in their stomach searing the butterflies they normally would feel for this guy.

"You heard what I said. I'm done trying to please you. I'm done trying to protect you. We're not even together and you think you can act like you control me? Like you have any power over when and where I can be out? You didn't have the right to do that when we *were* together. Screw that! Screw *you*. I will no longer, in fact, be *screwing you*."

Ben opens his mouth to, no doubt, shush them again, but Alex beats him to it.

"Yes, I know, *shh*!" They roll their eyes.

"And you know what else? I didn't ruin your senior year, *Benjamin O'Brien*. You did. We could've had the best time at prom! We could've gone out on *real dates*. None of that was *my fault*. And I completely respect that everyone comes out when they're ready. But the *least* you can do is take accountability for all this being *your* decision and having *nothing to do with me*."

Alex shakes their head, struggling to keep their voice even. "I don't know why I let you hold me back, Ben! I'm *proud* to be me."

Alex presses their hand against their chest, right above the broken heart that has only now started to sew itself back together. They know one badass confrontation isn't enough to fully heal it all at once, but it's a heck of a start.

Riding the same adrenaline boost, Alex continues, "I *value* myself. So I won't let you blame me for how difficult it is to stay in the closet. I came out a long time ago. And I'm not going back. For anyone."

With that, Alex turns on their heel and heads back. But before they reach the girls, they turn around again.

"Oh, and Ben?"

Ben, still rooted in the same spot, replies with, "Yeah?"

"Don't worry about me being secretly in love with you anymore."

Chapter 10: Jaya

JAYA WATCHES ALEX COME back. She also sees Ben scurry out the store exit, head ducked as if hiding from everyone. To be honest, he is. Most people could hear what was happening by the end of the conversation. Including Jaya and Duri.

The store isn't *that* big.

"That was the best thing I've ever seen!" Duri exclaims.

After Alex sits again, Duri shakes their shoulder vigorously. She's practically vibrating with exhilaration, almost as if she'd been the one telling Ben off instead of Alex.

Alex fluffs up their afro as they finally let loose the smile they've apparently been trying to fight. It radiates across their face like sunshine at dawn. This is a new day for Alex. A new time. And they're only going to keep rising into the sky, ready to shine and show the world their light.

Jaya doesn't actually say that.

But she claps a little for Alex and says, "I'm proud of you. You should be proud of yourself, too. That took guts!"

Alex does a little bow despite being seated on the ground.

"Thank you very much. You're both *literally* the best." Then they stop joking as they look between the two girls. "Seriously, though. I don't think I would've been able to do that. You know, if we hadn't talked things out. It also helped that I had an audience."

They remove their glasses so they can dab at the edge of their slightly wet eyes. Then they look at the pads of their fingers to make sure no mascara or eyeliner came off. Satisfied, they sniff and put their glasses back on.

"I've always been one to enjoy theatrics," Alex adds.

"You're a walking stereotype," Duri says with a chuckle.

Alex points at Duri. "You're thinking flamboyant gay guy. Now, I may be queer, but I'm not a guy. And I'm just naturally dramatic." Pretending their hair is longer than it actually is, Alex moves their right hand as if flipping their hair over their shoulder.

"Point taken," Duri replies respectfully. "What are you going to do now?"

Alex hums for a few seconds. They're clearly considering what they want to say before replying.

"I'm going to embrace singlehood for a while. Date myself and all that. I mean, look at me. Anyone would be lucky to date me. Even me." They fluff up their afro again as the girls laugh. Then Alex adds, "And when I'm ready, I think I'll check out Qupid."

"What's that?" Duri asks.

"It's a dating app for queer people looking for a serious relationship."

"What? I didn't know that was a thing!"

Jaya's about to open her mouth to say something, but she doesn't know what. It's not like she's ever dated before.

She's contemplating whether to suggest at least moving the conversation to another store—she'd do anything for a soda right now—when someone squeezes her shoulder. It's a smaller hand than the average adult and it's slightly sticky. If Jaya hadn't recognized the pressure and scent of melted ice cream, she would've moved out of the stranger's reach so fast she might've hurt herself.

"Karib?" Jaya asks as she turns around to face him. "What are you—"

Sure enough, Karib is behind her. But so is someone else in a familiar bright yellow romper.

"*Amma?*"

"Jaya," her mom replies in her brisk British accent. Her eyes bounce from teenager to teenager in confusion. "I don't recognize these friends of yours. Do they go to your school?"

"Uh," Jaya says as she scrambles to her feet, almost dropping her phone. She shoves it in her pocket, panic seizing her throat, though she's unsure why. It's not like she's in trouble or anything.

So why does it feel like she is?

Jaya briefly wonders why she hadn't heard her phone ring. Neither of her family members is big on texting. Her mom prefers phone calls and Karib, well, he mainly uses his phone to play *Pokémon GO*.

More than likely? Her mom and Karib just got off the ride and saw her sitting in the store. They wouldn't have had time to call her. And it *is* about time they got off the ride.

Since the single rider line moves faster, Jaya left her family behind in the regular line pretty quickly, especially considering the regular line is always longer for such a popular ride. Jaya usually prefers the single rider line when she's not with a friend from school. That way, Jaya can get through the line faster and try to calm her introverted nerves by reading an eBook on her phone while she waits for her family.

Obviously, things worked out differently today.

"No," Jaya finally replies. "We actually just met in line. *Amma*, this is Alex and that's Duri." She indicates each friend as she says their names. "Alex, Duri, this is my mom."

"Well, nice to meet you, Alex and Duri. Call me Indali."

"Nice to meet you as well, ma'am," Alex replies. They stand up, brushing their hands off on their pants.

"Right, yeah, same," Duri chimes in as she imitates Alex. Once she's on her feet, she says, "We've just been keeping Jaya company until you were done."

Indali smiles at the two teenagers. "How sweet of you. Thank you for entertaining my daughter." She places a loving hand on Jaya's forearm for a moment. "Though I'm sure she would've kept herself entertained with her silly little writing ideas. She's always taking notes on that phone of hers."

Jaya wraps her arms around herself. Indali's right. That was exactly what Jaya had done. Exhausted from trying to figure out how to break the news to her mom, Jaya spent most of the time in line brainstorming. She was writing down her asexual mermaid idea when Duri and Alex first grabbed her.

Did that really happen only a couple of hours ago? It seems like they've known each other for so much longer.

Jaya feels both of her friends' gazes on her, heavy as weights, calling her attention. She doesn't need to make eye contact. She knows it's because of the "silly little writing ideas" comment. Only her friends know how much it hurts.

"Karib, is it?" Duri asks.

"Yup," he replies in a bored voice.

He was just about to wipe his hands on a beach towel with the Black Hole Planet logo that's hanging behind him. But Indali cuts him a "Don't even *think* about it" look. So Karib opts for wiping his hands on his cargo shorts instead.

"Let me guess," Duri continues, gesturing to the character on his shirt. "Big *Star Trek* fan, huh?"

Jaya mentally facepalms. Of *course*. That's where the image on Ben's t-shirt is from as well.

At Duri's words, Karib stands at attention like a soldier. His sneakers squeak on the floor in the process.

"Yeah! Are you?"

Duri crosses her arms. "I might be. Why don't we go debate *Star Trek* vs. *Star Wars,* so we can give your mom and sister some privacy to talk?"

Alex groans. "Do I have to stay at the kids' table?"

"Yes," Duri replies dryly.

She leads Alex and Karib to the noisy toy section so Jaya can talk to Indali in peace. The last thing Jaya hears before they're out of earshot is Duri encouraging Karib to start the debate.

Jaya knows this is her invitation to confront her mom. To do what Alex did and face the person behind her biggest emotional struggle. But she can't move. She forces herself to take in a few deep breaths while her mom breaks the silence between them.

"They seem nice," Indali says, not taking her deep brown eyes off the two new people around her son. "I can't believe you three just met today. They seem so comfortable around you." She smiles warmly at her daughter. "It's nice to see you making new friends."

"Uh-huh," Jaya lets out. "Thanks, yeah."

Another beat.

"So, what did you want to talk about?"

"What?"

Indali raises one of her eyebrows, the same thick ones both Jaya and Karib inherited. "That girl. Sorry, what was her name again?"

"Duri."

"Ah, yes. Duri. She said something about us talking in private?"

Jaya doesn't know whether she should feel relief for Duri's help in setting up this conversation or annoyance. Is an amusement park gift shop really the best place for a life altering conversation with your mom about college and your future career?

Probably not, but Jaya knows herself. If she doesn't take advantage of the pressure she feels now, then she might wait until it's too late.

Besides, Duri went through all that trouble... clever girl.

Jaya swallows and presses her chewed nails into her palms. Then she forces out the words she's been wanting to say for months.

"I got accepted into Dartmouth College for their English program and I got a full ride because of a scholarship and I want to be a fantasy author."

Jaya opens her eyes, not having realized she'd shut them tightly as she rushed out her confession. Her mom stares back at her, completely dumbfounded.

"What?"

"Uh, do I need to say that again?"

Indali shakes her head. "No, I heard you. I'm just not sure I understood you correctly." She rubs her temples with her fingers. "Where is all this coming from?"

Jaya's about to reply when Indali gestures towards Duri and Alex, who are both now animated in conversation with Karib.

"What ideas did these two put in your head? Of course, I want you to make new friends, *chinna*, but you did just meet them. I'm not sure if they—"

"No," Jaya interrupts, something she doesn't think she's ever done before. She braces herself.

She'll never know what her mom wasn't sure about. But if Jaya doesn't continue, she'll lose her nerve. So, hands shaking in her dress pockets, she pushes on.

"Sorry, but that wouldn't even make any sense. This isn't, like, an idea I just had. I literally applied. I got the scholarship. And, well, I've accepted. This happened like a while ago."

"I suppose that's true," Indali says half-heartedly. "Sorry. I shouldn't have assumed." Her face relaxes somewhat, the wrinkles around her eyes seeming less pronounced. "Please don't think I'm not proud of you. Dartmouth is a fantastic school! I just wish you hadn't gone behind my back. Also, I thought you were going to the University of Florida."

Jaya takes in a deep breath through the upturned nose she got from her mom. Jaya holds the breath in her belly like something precious, filling her stomach with air. With courage. She wants to say this next part with no hesitations, stammering or stuttering. To be clear. To stand up for herself in the most respectful way possible. She lets out the breath with a big sigh.

Here we go.

"I know," Jaya says as she takes hold of one of her mom's hands. "And I'm sorry. UF is a great school. But I can't give up this opportunity! Imagine the kinds of writers I'll network with. The experienced professors who I'll learn from. I might graduate with a book deal for all we know!"

Jaya says this last sentence as an attempt for comic relief, but it's not until the words are out that she realizes it could happen. The possibilities are endless, causing her entire body to prickle with excitement. It's a subtle, yet distinct, improvement in how nervous she's been ever since she accepted Dartmouth's offer.

That is, until Jaya sees the crestfallen look on her mom's face.

"Oh my," Indali says, covering her face with shaking hands. "You're going to be reading poetry by the side of the road and collecting money in your guitar case!" Her hands partially muffle her voice, but the comment is still audible.

Jaya can't help but laugh. She doesn't even write poetry. And she hasn't played the guitar in years. In fact, she's pretty sure her beginner's guitar is just collecting dust under Karib's bed at this point. He begged her for it when she stopped playing, but he never practices either.

Normally, Indali's comments paralyze her daughter with anxiety. But after spending the morning with Duri and Alex, Jaya's having a slightly different outlook on things.

It's like maybe these fears of disappointing her mom or failing to achieve her dream aren't the end of the world. Because at least she believed in herself enough to try. That's really all she can ask.

Maybe her mom can try as well.

"*Amma*," Jaya says to Indali's neatly trimmed nails.

When she gets no response, Jaya gently pries her mom's hands away from her face. For a moment, Indali keeps her gaze down at her sandals. Then she meets her daughter's gaze with reddening eyes.

"Oh, *Amma*," Jaya chokes out.

She's never been good at seeing her mom cry. It's bad enough Jaya had to see Indali cry after the divorce. Back when Jaya was nine years old and Karib was three.

Jaya hadn't taken the divorce that badly. She saw it coming, watching helplessly as her parents distanced themselves until they were just roommates. Then the house was always quiet because they never communicated with one another.

What Jaya would've given to even hear them fight, which is what her friends with divorced parents usually experienced. But not Jaya. Hence, learning to fill the time with books while using her dad's old stereo to play Disney music, or her mom's Sonu Nigam CDs, in the background.

It was almost a relief when her parents divorced. It was amicable enough with no long custody battle. She and Karib stay with their mom throughout the school year. Then they spend the summers with their dad in Cali. Their dad is still involved the rest of the year too. Texting his kids almost every day. Talking to them on the phone or via video chat at least once a week.

The most annoying part?

When they're with their mom, Karib looks out of place. His skin is as light as their dad's, taking after the Caucasian side of the family. And when they're with their dad, Jaya's the odd one out. But that's about it.

Sure, they wish they could have both their parents in one place, but therapy helped Jaya address her feelings of blame for the divorce. And Karib was too young to remember what it was like to have their parents together. Jaya doesn't know if he'll need therapy someday, but he seems fine for now.

So, Jaya and Karib really *are* okay with the separation.

Not their mom, though.

Indali still feels the financial strain of being divorced with two kids, even with child support. And sometimes Jaya even overhears her mom on the phone with Jaya's *ajji* back in London, talking about how difficult it is to date as a single mother. Jaya's heart breaks for her mom to this day.

"Oh, *chinna*," Indali says as she runs a hand over her daughter's hair. "I know I'm being melodramatic. I'm just worried about you."

"But why?" Jaya asks.

Indali sighs. "It is hard enough to be a woman making your way alone in this world. But you're a woman of color. You have your father's eyes, but otherwise you're like me. Too much like me, actually."

She sniffles and smiles a little. Eyes watering too, Jaya takes hold of Indali's hand again.

"I didn't know you were worried about that, *Amma*. I wish you'd told me sooner." Indali raises an eyebrow and Jaya chuckles. "Touché. *I* should've told *you* sooner." It's her turn to sigh. "I was just scared. You're always talking about picking a sensible major and dependable career and making a home for myself."

"Yes," Indali interjects. "There is that as well. I know not all asexual people stay single. But if you do? It is even *more* important that you can take care of yourself. I want you to be okay and happy."

Alex's comment rings in Jaya's ears. "But they want to see me happy."

"I want to be happy too," Jaya replies now. "And I am. But this will make me happier in the future."

She swallows the lump in her throat, preparing for the rest of what she's going to say.

"Can you just trust me, *Amma*? Please? Like at least try. You've trusted me for almost eighteen years. I always finish my homework on time. Get immaculate grades. Participate in after-school programs. Never stay out late. Always babysit. And I do all my chores. You know me. I can do this."

She says this last sentence with more conviction than she actually feels, but she hopes if she says it enough, she'll believe it.

"And if I can't? Then maybe I can teach English or something. I don't know. This is scary. It's a lot of change and I could use your support. Because I want to figure it out. And you're right, *Amma*. I *am* like you. But if I'm half the woman you are, then I'm actually going to be pretty okay."

Indali waits a moment, letting her daughter's words sink in. It's almost painful how long she takes to respond. Jaya's about to say something, anything, when she gets a reply.

"I was wrong. You are more like your father than I thought."

"Really?" Jaya beams. "How so?"

Indali gives a half smile. "You both know how to get through to my heart."

Chapter 11: Duri

"DON'T BE TOO LONG," Indali says. "We still have plenty to do at the park today."

She puts an arm around Karib's shoulders and gives him a squeeze. He squirms out of her grasp, but his grin is so wide that Duri can see both his top and bottom rows of teeth.

"Next on the schedule," Karib says with a gleam in his brown eyes. "Martian Nuggets."

Duri smiles at the reminder of the little alien shaped chicken nuggets sold at the Meet Me at Mars fast-food restaurant on the other side of the park. She and Hana used to love those.

"Yes," Indali adds. "And I still need to go grocery shopping this afternoon. We're out of curry leaves and I want to make some *majjige huli* later."

"Okay, I'll catch up with you soon," Jaya promises. "I just want a chance to say goodbye to my new friends."

Disappointment drops into Duri's stomach, catching her by surprise. She can't even fight the frown that her lips are naturally turning into. She doesn't want her time with Jaya and Alex to end. This has been the most fun she's had in a while without Marí.

Having a girlfriend is great, but Duri hadn't realized how much she wished for a set group of friends. Real friends. People she could talk to about more than just attending GSA meetings. Or tips to shave off a few seconds on her running time.

It still amazes her. That she connected like this with two people she's only known for a few hours.

Wait...

Duri checks the time on her phone. Sure enough, it's past lunchtime. *Shit!* She'd only banked on having enough time to come to the park, go on her favorite ride, and get back home before her family returned from their post-service lunch.

And of course, her phone shows multiple notifications over the home screen picture of her and Marí.

Duri really needs to turn off Silent Mode on her phone when she's at an amusement park. She can't believe she's got so many missed calls from her mom. There are also a few from her dad, and a countless number of text messages from her sister.

How could Duri have completely lost track of time?

Her stomach growls, seconding the thought.

Duri's mind wanders towards food for a while, so she's only half listening when Jaya catches her and Alex up on what happened with Indali. Duri gets the gist, though. She tunes completely back into the conversation just as Jaya turns towards Duri.

"I can't thank you enough," Jaya says with the most relaxed smile. "Both of you."

"You're the one who did all the hard work," Alex replies. "Now it's my turn to be proud of you, Jay!"

Jaya somehow manages to both beam and shy away at the compliment.

Duri wants to be a good sport. So she goes to clap Jaya on the back for a job well done. Her hand stops midair, though, when she hears it. A voice so similar to her own, it can only come from one person.

"I *knew* you'd be here!"

Alex lowers their glasses down the bridge of their nose as if needing to see clearer. Obviously, Duri knows it's just for dramatic effect since, again, the glasses don't have any lenses.

Alex lets out a low whistle before saying, "Well, well, if it isn't Duri #2."

"*Excuse* me?"

Duri turns around and finds exactly who she expects. Hana, wearing a colorful floral skirt and a loose white blouse with matching wedges. She's standing with a hand propped on one of her hips and a BTS purse over her shoulder. Her eyes narrow at Alex, reddish-orange eyeshadow on her eyelids.

"Not that it's any of your business, but I'm five minutes older."

"Ooh," Alex replies as they put their glasses back in place. They hook their thumbs through the front belt loops of their pants. "Did someone turn down the AC? Because it just got chilly in here."

Jaya lets out a little giggle at the clever response before Hana turns her icy glare on Duri's second friend. Jaya quickly presses her lips together and looks away.

"Hana," Duri says, wanting to protect her friends. "Stop."

"Whatever," Hana scoffs, pouting her pink glossed lips. "Here, Mom and Dad were *so* worried about your '*cold*'. You know they almost went straight home after church? Instead of going out to lunch?" She twists her dark brunette braid around her index finger.

"I knew you were BSing, though, so I convinced them otherwise." Tilting her head, she raises an eyebrow colored with eyebrow pencil. "Imagine the surprise when we get home to find that my baby sister wasn't where she said she'd be."

"Oh, grow up, Han," Duri replies with a growl.

Her eyes shift to Jaya and Alex then and, realizing the show she's putting on, Duri stomps away from her friends. As she does so, she grabs Hana's arm and drags her away. Duri stops when they get to the "Astronauts Only" door where staff occasionally bring out inventory.

Hana pulls her elbow out of Duri's grasp and fixes the strap of her purse, which had fallen off her shoulder.

"Hypocrite," Hana mutters as she blows a stray strand of hair out of her eyes. Duri rubs her hands over her face in frustration.

"Well, *sorry*," Duri replies, dropping her hands in a huff. "Guess we're less identical than we thought."

"And what do you mean by *that*?"

Duri shrugs. "Because I'm not perfect like my oh-so-wise five minutes older than me sister."

"Here we go again," Hana says. She rolls those identical brown eyes that Duri has.

Duri takes in a deep breath to avoid snapping with another sassy response. If Alex could face their ex and Jaya could confront her mom, then Duri can have an actual conversation with her sister. Duri lets out the breath and does something she hasn't done with Hana since they were in middle school.

She decides to be vulnerable.

"I'm jealous, okay?"

Hana, about to say something, stops in her tracks. After an almost unbearable second, she says, "What?"

Duri puts her hands in her back pockets and looks down at her pink sneakers and purple socks.

"Everything comes so easily to you. Good grades. Friends. Dancing. And you know what to study in college. Plus, you're going to one of the best schools." She swallows. "Congrats, by the way. I don't think I told you."

Duri's jaw snaps shut then. She can't bring herself to say anything else. She can't remember the last time she felt *this* uncomfortable.

To her surprise, Hana laughs. Duri's head snaps up to meet her sister's amused gaze. For some reason, seeing Hana's dimples as she laughs makes Duri want to explode. But before Duri can let loose the insult that springs to her tongue, Hana waves her hands in front of her.

"I'm not laughing at you," Hana swears. "Not really." She settles down and sighs. "Thanks, but you're only partially right. Sure, I like to study. And I'm definitely a social butterfly. But performance dance takes a lot of work. And... and I've told no one this. But... well, I actually *don't* know what I want to major in. Like literally not a clue."

Duri's eyebrows shoot up into her bangs. "What? I thought you were studying biology. Isn't science your thing? Like Dad."

The twins' dad works as a general practitioner, so it has always thrilled him to see any interest in the sciences from his daughters. Their mom is a software programmer, though. With women being so rare in the technology field, she hoped one of her daughters would take an interest in coding or computers.

Apparently, neither has come true yet.

Hana shrugs before responding.

"One," she says as she raises her index finger. "Just because you're good at something doesn't mean you need to make it your career. Two." She makes a peace sign. "I only liked science because it makes sense to me. And three." She holds up three fingers. "I had to pick *something* to major in if I wanted my application to be taken seriously at an Ivy League school."

The twins are silent for a moment, neither of them knowing what else to say. Hana, like usual, breaks the silence first.

"We were pretty obsessed with sci-fi for a while." She looks around at the space themed store. "And this place. Remember how Mom was afraid of this ride?"

A smile tugs at Duri's lips. "Of course I remember."

She always wondered why her dad didn't just leave his wife drinking coffee or eating a pastry at the Cosmos and Comets Cafe next door to the Galactic Survival ride. Duri now realizes that she and Hana were probably too young to ride alone back then. Or to be split up as single riders.

Huh. Well, how's that for irony? After all, this conversation between Duri and her sister wouldn't even be happening if it weren't for the single rider line today.

Duri swears God must have a weird sense of humor.

Hana lets out a wistful sigh. "I kind of miss that. Don't you?"

"Miss what? Playing rock-paper-scissors to see who had to sit with Mom and put up with her praying on the ride?"

The twins share a surprisingly easy laugh as they reminisce.

Hana clarifies, "Not that. But I miss when life was simpler."

Duri nods. Hana's not wrong. Isn't that exactly why Duri skipped church for Black Hole Planet in the first place?

Hana continues, "There weren't as many expectations back then, you know? To, like, get ready to adult. Mom and Dad just wanted us to be kids."

Duri scrunches up her nose. "Maybe for you. But Mom and Dad don't really care about me anymore."

Hana scrunches up her nose too. "I don't know where you got *that* idea, but they never stopped caring about you."

Duri shakes her head. "If that's true, then why did they stop having high hopes for me?"

"Seriously?" Hana says in disbelief. "They're always telling me how much they wish you'd do something with your life. They just don't know how to get you to do it. Why do you think I'm so hard on you?"

"I just thought you were a hardass."

"Only because I know you can do it! I *know* you can prove everyone wrong. That you'll surprise us all one day and do something amazing."

Duri's mouth goes dry. She licks her lips a few times, too stunned to make them form words. She had no idea her parents still had dreams for her behind closed doors. And she *definitely* didn't know her sister thought so highly of her.

"Th-thank you," Duri finally stammers.

A blush spreads across the soft skin of Hana's round face. Duri assumes all those Korean face masks that her sister likes to order online have done their job.

"No problem," Hana replies at last.

After a moment, Duri mutters, "I wish I believed in myself that much."

She recalls Jaya's words. "It sounds like you might have AD-HD."

"Oh, Duri," Hana says in a soft voice. "I'm jealous of you too, you know."

Duri chokes on a laugh. When she catches her breath, she asks, "What would you *possibly* have to be jealous of?"

Hana leans her shoulder against the wall. "Because you're brave. You don't let Mom or Dad or me get to you. I can't even imagine telling them that both their daughters have no idea what to do with their lives."

Duri's heart, which usually constricts with anxiety when she's around her twin, warms her entire chest. Beneath all the anger she's held for Hana, Duri didn't realize how much she still cared about her sister.

Reaching out a shaky hand, Duri takes hold of one of Hana's and says something she hasn't said in years. "I have your back."

Hana waits a beat and then grips Duri's hand. "And I have yours."

One more squeeze. Then the girls let go.

To have some comic relief, Duri smirks and adds, "So, you're saying you want to *collab*?"

Hana snorts back a laugh. "You are seriously the *worst* Gen Z-er I know."

Duri winks as a response. Marí playfully tells her that all the time.

A short, awkward pause happens then between the twins. Duri knows she has to say what's on her mind. Otherwise, she might forget. And for once, she'd actually appreciate someone keeping her accountable.

So, without breaking eye contact, she says, "I think I might have ADHD."

"Really?" Hana asks. She plays with one of her gold hoop earrings, a habit she always does when she's thinking over something. "Huh. That... that makes sense." Then, almost mumbling to herself, she says, "Might be worth looking into."

Duri's ears perk up at that. She didn't realize how worried she'd been about Hana's response until she heard it.

"Right? I think I will. My new friends actually suggested it."

Duri looks over her shoulder, only to find Jaya and Alex failing to hide behind a nearby keychain rack. After realizing Duri caught them, the two pretend to be overly interested in some rocket shaped keychains. Duri shakes her head, chuckling to herself.

"Hey," Hana says, calling back Duri's attention. "Are we okay? You and me?"

Duri nods in agreement, and plans to say so, but she surprises herself by saying, "I'm sorry."

Hana, clearly surprised as well, blinks her long lashes a few times.

"I'm sorry too," she finally responds.

Neither Duri nor Hana clarify what they're apologizing for, but Duri knows they both understand. It's an apology for not understanding each other before. And making assumptions. And words that should've never been said.

Then, as the biggest surprise of the day, Hana steps forward and wraps her arms around Duri.

The sisters hug for a minute, somewhat uncomfortably at first. But then they relax into the embrace. It's like muscle memory kicks in, reminding Duri of all the times they hugged as kids and preteens. Duri can't even remember the last time she touched Hana before today, let alone held her.

As the twins separate, they give each other small smiles.

Duri imagines that it's still going to take time to figure out how to act like sisters again. But she's willing to give it a shot if Hana is. And Duri has to admit, it's a weight off her shoulders to know she has someone in her corner again.

It reminds Duri of being bullied in elementary school. Like when her classmates made fun of her for making impulsive comments in class. Hana never hesitated to stand up for her. How could Duri have forgotten little details of their sisterhood like that?

She supposes years of miscommunication and animosity can do that to anyone.

A tear escapes the corner of Duri's eye, and Hana wipes it away with the knuckle of her index finger. Duri grins and sniffles.

"Well," Duri says, "aren't we just a couple of cliché sisters?"

"I guess so," Hana replies warmly. "Hey. Want to go on Galactic Survival for old time's sake? Before we go home?" Hope flashes in Hana's eyes as she adds, "Mom and Dad *did* already pay for my ticket. Might as well get our money's worth before facing their wrath."

Duri groans. She can picture it already.

The disappointed look on her dad's face as he mutters to himself about wishing he had a son. Her mom's infamous hypocritical speech about Duri's behavior going against traditional Korean values, even though her mom was born in the US and is almost as Americanized as the twins.

Duri doesn't even want to think about what's waiting for her at home. But maybe it won't be so bad with her sister by her side.

Plus, even Hana's rebelling a little. Their parents probably told Hana to bring her sister back as soon as possible. In fact, Duri's positive they told Hana that this isn't a pleasure trip.

Just the idea of Hana pushing their boundaries for her sister makes Duri's heart squeeze with love.

Ugh, just wait until Marí hears about this. Duri can already hear the lighthearted teasing. Her girlfriend will never let her live this down.

Once Duri gets out of her head again, she agrees to Hana's plan. She *did* use a good chunk of her allowance to buy her ticket and, technically, still hasn't used it.

"Let's get something to eat after," Duri adds. "I'm starving."

She knows she's going to be grounded, which means no eating out. And she'll probably be eating a lot of homemade *kimchi* in the meantime.

With this in mind, Duri suggests, "We can get Martian Nuggets."

Hana gasps a little. "I haven't had those in *forever*."

She moves towards the door, which Duri takes as approval for her idea. But before Hana can get far, Duri stops her.

"I have to let my friends know I'm heading out."

Hana nods. "I'll save us a place in line. Text me?"

"Deal."

Hana starts to leave the store, but stops when she passes by Alex. They've given up pretending to be interested in the keychain rack. And they're not trying to hide anymore, either.

Jaya also stopped looking at the keychains and instead stands by Alex, nervously chewing on her pinky nail.

"I probably owe you an apology," Hana says. "I was pretty rude when we met."

Alex looks a bit taken aback. "I accept your apology," they reply, "but I don't need it. I respect your sass."

"Thanks," Hana says, blushing. She makes eye contact with Duri. "I like this one." Then she points at Jaya with an acrylic nail. "I haven't heard much from you, but if Duri likes you, then you're okay in my book." Jaya stops chewing her pinky nail as Hana adds, "Sorry for basically ignoring you when I got here."

"It's okay," Jaya replies with a smile. Then Hana heads out again.

But Duri has another realization. And she wants to say it before she forgets. Not bothering to run across the store, Duri cups her hands around her mouth.

"Hey, Han!"

"Yeah?!" Hana replies loudly, turning around even though she has the door open.

"We'll figure it all out!" Duri shouts, ignoring the staff and shoppers who are eyeing her like she's the world's biggest weirdo. "We're Seongs! Success is literally our name!"

Duri says this, trying to be cheeky. But as she watches Hana flash a dimpled smile, Duri wonders why she never thought about herself that way before.

Hana finally gives a little wave to the three teenagers. Then she closes the tinted glass door behind her. Jaya and Alex wave back a little too late as they take the final few steps towards Duri.

Alex is the first to speak. "We're not even going to pretend we didn't hear everything."

"Especially that last part," Jaya adds, wincing a little.

Duri chuckles. "It's fine. Saves me time explaining." Jaya lets out a little sigh of relief, as if she expected Duri to be mad about the eavesdropping. But Duri couldn't care less. She was going to tell them everything, anyway.

"In that case," Alex replies, "let me be the first to say Mazel Tov."

"I'm happy for you," Jaya adds.

"And I'm glad to hear you're going to be there for each other now."

Duri shrugs, but she can't deny the hope inflating in her chest. "We're going to try at least."

"Right," Alex says as they fidget with their nose ring. "I'm an only child. What do I know?"

"No worries," Duri replies.

Then the three of them stand around without saying anything for a while.

Duri watches as a married couple gets in line at the cash register. The cashier rings up the people ahead of them. Then greets the couple with fake enthusiasm, like Matt. Duri can't believe they both still have jobs. Even she could do that.

Who knows? Maybe someday soon she will.

"Well," Alex finally says, drawing Duri's attention back to her friends. "I should probably get going. See what my dads want to do about lunch." Alex takes their fake glasses off and pockets them. Then they add, "I guess this is it."

"I suppose so," Jaya replies sadly.

Then Duri says what she knows everyone must be thinking. "Oh, come on! Nobody died. We can stay in touch." She pulls out her phone and waves it in the air. "We have these, remember? And TikTok?"

Alex gives another one of their brilliant smiles. "I know. Just wanted to make sure you two felt the same. I've had enough unrequited affection for one day."

Jaya nods enthusiastically. "Thank God someone said something. I would've regretted leaving without getting everyone's phone number."

The teens swap numbers and say their goodbyes. After promising to text, they walk towards the store exit.

Right before they open the doors, though, Jaya says, "It's funny, isn't it?"

"What is, Jay?" Alex asks, coming to a stop. Duri rests her hand against the room temperature metal of the door handle as she waits.

Jaya clasps her hands, letting her arms dangle in front of her.

"Like we spent so long in the single rider line, feeling alone with our different life problems." Jaya hesitates, but Alex smiles warmly and Duri waves her free hand in encouragement. Jaya continues, "And we didn't realize we were in the company of future friends the entire time."

"So poetic," Duri replies with a smirk.

"True," Alex adds, placing their hand on one of Jaya's shoulders. "I, for one, am really glad we met."

"Me too," Jaya says as Alex squeezes her shoulder. Then the teens gaze at Duri, waiting for her to agree.

Duri looks down at Jaya. Then up at Alex. Two people she didn't know existed when she woke up this morning. People she wants in her life moving forward. Her eyes land on a floor-length mirror behind Jaya and Alex. Duri sees herself, spending time with two new friends, and she likes what she sees.

Because isn't that the point of friendship? To have people who cheer you on as you try to get your life on track? *And* who run the track side-by-side with you?

Returning her gaze back to Alex and Jaya, Duri finally replies, "Me three."

Author's Note

IN JULY 2022, I FOUND myself in a single rider line at an amusement park by myself. I'd never gone alone before then, but I was free and had an annual pass.

So, why not, right?

This particular ride sat two people per row. That means I wasn't thrown in with an uneven number of family members. Like Duri, Alex, and Jaya, the ride attendant paired me with one person from the regular line.

However, unlike Duri, Alex, and Jaya, I didn't become instant best friends with someone I just met in line. I know that's not very realistic anyway, but I *did* try to start a conversation.

After we got on the roller coaster, any awkwardness was gone. We screamed as the ride went backwards. Laughed when we got scared. Shouted and whooped our heads off.

Once it was over, we spent the entire time talking while we walked to the exit. We gushed over how fun the ride was. Shared what our favorite parts were. Agreed that getting the front row was lucky.

Then we were back in the general area of the park and the awkwardness returned. We just didn't know how to say goodbye.

So, we didn't.

As we went our separate ways, an idea formed. This stranger and I shared an experience. The first time they went on this ride. The first time I went on this ride alone. I'll never forget the memory even if we didn't learn each other's names.

But what if we had?

Questions flooded my brain. What if you met the love of your life in a single rider line? Or what if that's how you met your best friend? What if that complete stranger ended up being an integral part of your journey? And what if that person appeared at the perfect moment in your life?

That's how *Single Riders: A YA Novella* was born.

You see. There was another reason why I'd gone to the park by myself.

Okay, a few reasons.

Like Duri, I was running from my problems. Like Alex, I was grieving an unexpected change in a romantic relationship. And like Jaya, I was isolating myself from those who supported me the most.

So, I wrote the story fueled by my anxiety and grief. I wrote the story for my current mental state, but also for the mental health of the teenager I used to be. That teenager who thought life would get easier. That teenager beginning to understand her intersectional identity and how that correlated with her dreams.

Needless to say, I finished the first draft of this book in one weekend. And the longer I spent revising it, the longer the story became. Until this novelette turned into a novella.

Now, even though I wrote this story for myself, I also wrote it for you.

I wrote it for every queer reader who's tired of seeing the same old representation of the LGBTQIA community in books. Because, no, we're not all Caucasian cisgender gays or lesbians. And yes. We are more than just our sexual orientation.

I wrote it for every reader labeled as "diverse" in real life who doesn't see that diversity in the main characters of books. And I wrote it for every reader who yearns for more stories about platonic love and friendship beyond childhood.

Finally, I wrote it for every reader who enjoys quick, fun, and heartwarming stories.

That reader is me. And you.

I hope these characters came to life for you as they did for me. That they cursed aloud the same frustrations you struggle with. Reminded you of your worth and that of those around you. Whispered truths about yourself that you hadn't realized existed.

Because they did for me. I fell in love with Duri, Alex, and Jaya the more I learned about them. These three were born and reborn in my mind until they took full shape. And once they did? I never wanted to stop spending time with them.

They comforted me and, hopefully, you as well.

So, I hope you'll share this story. Leave a review on Amazon, BookBub, BookTok, Goodreads, StoryGraph, your own blog, or wherever. Help this indie author find like-minded readers. Share your opinions on social media and tag me so I can hear your thoughts.

Because your voice matters. And when you feel like it doesn't? In those moments when homophobic, transphobic, and/or xenophobic voices threaten to drown you out? Remember that you're not alone.

You're never as alone as you think.

Love, Selys

Acknowledgements

I HAVE TO THANK MY fellow BookTokers right away. At one of the loneliest points in my life, I found a community on TikTok that I never expected to find: BookTok.

No longer was I the only queer Latina author and/or reader. I wasn't the only one venting about the lack of racial diversity in books. Or the need for more kinds of representation for my fellow LGBTQIA peeps.

I connected with other readers like me. With authors completely unlike me. And vice versa. I opened my mind to an entire world beyond myself and what I usually read or wrote. And I learned about this wonderful and complicated universe made of books and genres that I didn't know existed.

BookTok brought back my mojo in more ways than one. I'd been in a reading slump and struggling with writer's block. Now I have a TBR list mostly made up of books written by indie authors. And I've written a whole new book. One that never would've occurred to me without all the different and thought-provoking opinions on BookTok.

On that note, I have to thank my beta readers, sensitivity readers, proofreaders, and ARC readers. Most of you came from BookTok, which completely blows my mind. If I had never downloaded that one app, I never would've found you.

Thank you for taking a chance on an indie author and her first YA novella. Your feedback and reviews have been incredibly helpful and motivational. This book wouldn't be what it is today, nor will it get to where it needs to be, without you.

And like every book I've written before and that I will write in the future, I want to thank my friends and family for supporting me. You were my first fan club and I love you all.

Lastly, I thank God. Whether God is genderless or not, a personification of love and all that is good or just the universe. It's my sense of spirituality that makes me believe I was put on this earth to help make it a little better than when I entered it.

What better way than through my writing? Even if it's just one book at a time.

Did you love *Single Riders: A YA Novella*? Then you should read *An Unconscious Mestiza: A Collection of Memoir Stories*[1] by Selys Rivera!

[2]

Puerto Rico, the US, PR, the United States, blurring the separation the Atlantic Ocean attempts to do to my blood. I'm a rope in a tug of war. I'm the border. I'm two places at once and yet neither of them entirely. If neither feels like mine, then how can it be sad?

Or maybe, that's exactly why it is.

The girl with the light skin, brown eyes, and straight, dark-brown hair, who speaks better English than Spanish. I realize

---

1. https://books2read.com/u/mdlgRR

2. https://books2read.com/u/mdlgRR

that, deep down, I'm not that different. Maybe I do belong after all.

I am *una mestiza.*

At just four years old, Selys Rivera's life had already changed forever. As her biological parents separated, she had to leave the comforts of her Puerto Rican homeland for the unknown landscape waiting for her in Massachusetts.

In *An Unconscious Mestiza: A Collection of Memoir Stories*, Selys Rivera openly shares her mental health challenges and grief as she tries to figure out what being Puerto Rican, American, and a woman means to her. Her shattered youth and move to a new culture created the challenges that she faces in these pages as the reader shares the stories that unfold into an intricate mosaic of a victorious life.

Powerful and relatable, Selys Rivera's memoirist debut is a reminder that just a little love, forgiveness, acceptance, and faith can go a long way toward healing and a true sense of wholeness.

Read more at https://www.selysrivera.com.

About the Author

Originally from Puerto Rico, Selys Rivera considers herself a queer, God-loving, and social justice-obsessed chica.

Selys has published articles, poems, and stories in magazines, anthologies, and literary journals, as well as books. Her favorite genres to write in are YA/NA Fiction, Memoir, and Poetry.

In her free time, you can find her reading too many books, spending time with loved ones, or playing with her red Dachshund named Ketchup.

Follow her on TikTok @SelysRiveraWrites to stay connected.

Author photo by Selys Rivera.

Read more at https://www.selysrivera.com.

Made in the USA
Coppell, TX
29 December 2023